ANCHOR OUT

ANCHOR OUT

A Novel

BARBARA SAPIENZA

SHE WRITES PRESS

Published 2017
Printed in the United States of America
Print ISBN: 978-1-63152-210-9
E-ISBN: 978-1-63152-211-6
Library of Congress Control Number: 2016957804

For information, address:
She Writes Press
1563 Solano Ave #546
Berkeley, CA 94707

Cover design © Julie Metz, Ltd./metzdesign.com
Interior design by Tabitha Lahr

She Writes Press is a division of SparkPoint Studio, LLC.

This is a work of fiction. Names, characters, places, and incidents either are the product of the author's imagination or are used fictitiously. Any resemblance to actual persons, living or dead, is entirely coincidental.

For Catherine Kurkjian, my sister

and

Sister Mary Neill

1

All Saints Day, November 1

At daybreak Frances lifts her head from her bed in the lower cabin of her sailboat to peek through a small round porthole at water's level at a sea lion swimming and pretends she's conversing with her early barks. Maybe she has a message that will dispel a relentless lethargy. But as soon as Frances comes more fully awake, the words seem scrambled and disappear like the receding tide. Through the porthole, she watches one dive and resurface in front of her neighbor Russell's boat, seventy-five feet portside. The pink morning light reflects off the sleek wet mammal. Is she calling for Russell to wake up? Frances wonders if the sea lion is drawing a line connecting her boat to his, maybe delivering a message about her yearnings. Her eyes stay glued to Russell's boat, looking for a sign that he has heard. She waits until she sees his head emerge from the lower cabin. She watches the way he rises out of the stairwell, head and then torso until he's in full view—all six feet of him—bringing her back to this glorious morning on Richardson Bay.

She feels joyful to be living on this piece of the bay anchored nearer the Belvedere side of the channel, only three hundred feet from the docks, yet worlds apart.

She watches Russell walk toward the stern of his thirty-foot sailboat, folding a tarp with his long sinewy hands, creasing it, brushing off the night residue. His wetsuit lies drying on the bow. Likely he's been in the water before daybreak. Perhaps he used that new headlamp he bought. He always tidies up, battening down the boards as they say, before going ashore for his day jobs. She watches how he combs his thinning hair, first with his fingers and then with the palm of his hand. His rowboat, outfitted with the new Yamaha engine, swags as he lowers in, unties it, and then pushes off.

He likes to tell his storm story to her or anybody within earshot. Last year it was *the* story at the Café Trieste, a corner bar and restaurant near the water's edge where the locals take their coffees and drink too many beers, telling their tales of woe and glory. Russell's tale was still topping their charts: his boat broke anchor in the middle of the night and dodged nearby crafts as he tried desperately to control it with the tiller. Remarkably, he didn't hit one of the many closely anchored boats, and finally managed to run aground safely onto a sandbar near Strawberry Point. Frances closes her eyes against the possibility of a storm taking her out to sea some night while she sleeps.

"Franny," Russell calls out, "Are you coming into town?" She pictures him sitting in his rowboat near her stern. She can hear his engine idling. He knows she's awake. She swears he can hear her breathing.

"Hi O, Franny!" he calls again. She hits her head, startled by the loudness of his voice. She rolls her feet onto the floor and takes the stairs slowly, stopping midway to peek out at the man she spends so much time thinking about. She watches him through the companionway, the entrance from the cabin to the cockpit, holding onto the rails. Russell has one hand on the tiller to keep the skiff steady as his engine idles a soft hum. She pokes her head out all the way, staring at him, trying to remember his question.

"I'll see you sooner or later, Russell," she says, rubbing the top of her head.

"The season's changing. That means heavy rains," he warns.

"And a big sea."

"You remember those gusts last January. They reached near a hundred miles an hour, Franny."

"I do. Nasty, nasty."

"You need to buy a second anchor just to be safe, and a new chain for that buoy." He looks out at her buoy, a rounded half bell bobbing in the current about fifteen feet from her boat. "And then there's that small engine on your dinghy. It's as unreliable as hell."

She walks toward the cockpit, straightening her thick hair with her fingers. Stopping in front of him, barefoot and in her sweats, she imagines gales gusting in the middle of the night and sending her crashing into the rocks on Belvedere Island, or worse, pulling her out under the Golden Gate Bridge. That would be real hell. Being adrift because an anchor breaks loose is her worst nightmare, yet she doesn't do the necessary chores to forestall this event. While she used to set sail frequently around the bay to Angel Island and back again to her anchorage, she's been lazier lately. Just thinking about it puts a weight on her shoulders. She shrugs to shake away this heavy feeling. Never mind preparing to sail, she doesn't even do the simple work needed to prepare for strong ebbs or a flood, like buy a new chain for her anchor. She shakes her head at her lack of motivation.

Oh, it's not just here in her boat that she slacks off; she hasn't painted or prayed to God for over ten years. Just thinking about not being ready for the coming storms, not doing her work of prayer, not painting, makes her head throb, sending a great heat that runs through her veins, making her want to jump overboard to feel the cold flush of water on her skin. She holds onto the gunwale at the edge of the deck.

"You okay, Franny?" Russell asks. "You have that far-away look." He pulls himself closer, holding her rope tightly between those long fingers, stretching his neck muscles tautly so she can see his tendons. She's close enough to touch his face, with its angled contour, but she resists. Oh, if she could only draw his beautiful outstretched neck, the two triangular muscles that caress the elongated one. Just that would suffice.

"I'm okay, just a little dizzy from the waves you're making, Russell," she teases him, reaching for the rail.

"I'll be heading to West Marine later. I can get some chain for your buoy anchor." She looks toward her rounded bobbing buoy, so red with the morning rays shining on it.

"Maybe you can check the old anchor first?" she suggests. "Then we'll know better if that girl has any life in her." She winks at him.

"Can do, tomorrow."

"You're kind to me, Russell," she acknowledges as he backs up and pulls away toward the public pier in Sausalito. She loves how he tends to her, offering to buy the lengths of chain to replace the old rusted one, to inspect the underside of the hull. He checks in almost daily. And how he's taken to calling her Franny, she loves that, too. It makes her feel sixteen again though she's sixty. How has this happened? At sixteen her life didn't hold the promise of a boy flirting and taking care of her. Was she so preoccupied with caring for her younger sister, her mother? What was it? What kept her? Boys were discouraged by her dad, but maybe he discouraged her from the boys too. In fact, he embarrassed her when she became interested in boys, telling her that dancing or wearing lipstick was vain, a sin even. She covers her mouth with her rough hand, feeling the scratch of the skin, remembering how her dad once scrubbed her lipstick off with an abrasive. Was that when Jimmy walked her home from school? She tastes a soapy film in her mouth.

And how is it that her choices have put her living three hundred feet from land out in the middle of the bay? Russell's closeness buoys her, though she wishes she knew more about his life story, which remains a bit of a mystery. He hasn't told her about his earlier times, leaving her wondering if he has a wife or children in the closet somewhere. Though attentive to her, he spends time cavorting with younger women in bars in the evenings. How can she ever imagine competing with them? She touches the roll of her tummy, the wiry hairs on her chin, the small bump on her head.

As he disappears from view, she sits down and turns to watch Otto, another neighbor, not more than four boat lengths away on her starboard side. He's bending over the wheel at the stern of his Lancer 30, a twin to her own boat. Otto is barrel-chested with a thin waist and wears woolen knickers in the cold mornings, an old carryover from his skiing days in

Norway. He reminds her of a Nordic Santa with his full white beard that complements his tweed knickers. Like her, he has ruddy flesh tones and blue eyes that twinkle like faraway stars. She imagines him swooshing down some alpine slope and laughs at the image of an old bearded elf on skis. But he wouldn't have been old then, likely he'd been pretty handsome as a young man.

Taking his time, he rolls up his bed cover. Did he sleep out on the deck? He places the neat roll in a sack, and then a duffle like he's stacking Russian dolls. He rubs his beard between tasks as if he's asking it what's the next thing for him to do. He mumbles something, or maybe he's praying. She can almost discern the whispers of his words carried by the gentle wind, or is it the water that magnifies sound out here? Then he leans out toward her and says in his Norwegian pitch, enunciating slowly in full voice, "Are you spying on me again?"

"I spy, you spy," she jests, then yells, "I'm admiring you, wondering if I'll be folding my blanket and rowing into town daily to make mischief when I'm eighty."

"You're making mischief now, Frances."

"Am I?"

"You're the trickster among us," he says. "See you in town."

•   •   •

The image of being the mischief-maker in this community of live-aboards intrigues her. She speaks aloud in a singsong voice, making up her own lyrics to the tune of "Popeye the Sailor Man." "Yup, we live in a boat anchored out, rent and tax free on federal 'land.' Anchor outs we are!" Her words dissolve in the sea breeze. "We're moored to a buoy—in Richardson Bay—like babies in a great sea cradle. Some of us drink—too much at Smitty's—then try to row back out in the dark." She stops herself at the sobering thought. One of her neighbors, a woman, drowned last week rowing back from town. Though managing to cross the channel, she missed her mark and never made it to her boat. And she had been so close. Is that what could happen to me? Frances covers her mouth as a prayer escapes her lips. *Lord, may she rest in peace. I know we are all brothers and sisters. There but for the grace of God go I.*

How easy the prayers come after so many years of prayer abstinence, slipping out of her mouth like baby teeth. Her hand rests on her soft cheek, remembering the solace of prayer, missing that ritual in her life. The longing she feels is for the early light reflecting through the stained-glass windows in the chapel where she prayed daily. Her knees rest on the padded bench; her arms in prayer on the wooden railing; the old nuns bend in front of her. Other novices beside her pray alone, yet they bow together in intimate consort with each other's souls. The great church with the high wooden ceilings, the sounds of wood creaking, offer the feeling of space and humility, maybe like the space of the water and sky does today.

She considers herself a monastic living on the water. No one else around here knows she was a nun for more than twenty years, nor do they know that the high wooden ceilings of basilicas are built like the hull of a ship. She cherishes this knowledge; this home on the water is her sanctuary. She remembers how as a child she'd run to St. Thomas' whenever Mama scolded and just sit under the timber eaves until her heart stopped racing. As an adult, the cathedral gave her solace until she was dismissed by Father Justin, who in the end had not supported her. Her solitude dissolves as she hears the voice of her Superior.

"Don't open that can of worms, Sister Frances. Why not teach them the facts, the facts will tell the story. They need details, not poetry and metaphor," he'd barked.

"You're right, Father, just the facts," she agreed. "They need to know about the new gospels found in Egypt, the gospels of Thomas and Philip and Mary Magdalene, so they can decide for themselves."

Her head spins even now as she pictures the great beast of a man in black, staring at her from the back of the classroom spewing angry silence, hands balled up into tight fists as she spoke to the freshman class about the new findings of Mary Magdalene.

"I am giving them the facts, Father. You just don't believe she was The Apostle of the Apostles." She banishes his explosive red face by looking out at the water, the great body of swelling motion eases her outrage at the preposterous man of antiquity. She breathes a great ocean breath into herself, tasting the salt, staring deeply into the vast pool around her as a female figure takes form. Sky-blue robes flow around the woman. Silky and ethereal, they fall to her feet gently cradling her, folding and unfolding with the rhythm of the sea. Frances hugs herself as she allows this image to soothe her restless soul. Thinking of the Virgin Mary as a whole woman, unified unto herself, gives her consolation.

Aren't I more like the Virgin Mary than not? Frances is, after all, a virgin in the spiritual sense of the word: captain of her own ship. And doesn't she have Russell and Otto as mates on either side of her craft? They honor her and let her be herself.

She waits in this blue splendor of the sea, watching the sun reflect pink on the white sides of the moored boats before going through the companionway and down to her cabin, where she lies on her bed listening to the water gently lap the boat, letting the early rays warm her. When she stretches her legs out fully under the woolen blanket, she kicks off *The Chronicle*, which lay draped over her bed, onto the cabin floor. She bends over to find the newspaper opened to the obituary page, where in bold black type she reads, "Alan Sterling, noted San Francisco painter and art teacher whose distinctive works have been widely exhibited internationally . . . died . . . " She stops, then bends closer to the fuzzy photograph as if she might see deeper into him. A young Alan faces her with his lips curled in a gentle bow. She imagines his eyes glowing blue. She touches the newsprint, rubbing the paper on her cheek, then plants a kiss on his small face. With her inky fingers she writes on the small round windowpane, *Don't leave me*. She feels a stinging sensation in her nose. She squints against the flood of sadness rising to her eyes.

Wide-awake now, she slips into her Nikes and grabs her blue slicker. She'll dress once she gets to town where she keeps a rented locker. Frances mentally picks out the tweed skirt and grabs her red woolen coat. She pulls the rope and watches her dinghy glide toward the stern. Once inside, she grips the oars, feeling their solidity as an extension of her own hands. The floppy floor of the dinghy vibrates under her feet as it rides ripples of water beneath. She hears the dripping water slide off the oars as a metronome in her heart, or are the drips flowing from her eyes and nose? She lets the water flow through her stinging nose, bringing tears to her eyes. Alan, the man who painted with her beloved grandfather, who encouraged her to pick up the paintbrush again, is dead. She can hear his voice. "Keep painting, Frances."

Where are you now, dear Alan, my beloved teacher? Have you too disappeared like my sister and my grandfather? She looks up to the sky whose light is changing, creating darks and lights like a great canvas.

·   ·   ·

"I'm on my way to Fort Mason, Jack," she says to the ferryman, drifting toward the main deck of the ferry near the concession stand, where people order their hot drinks. She waits in line watching the server.

"Where you off to so early?" asks Myrna as she pours the coffee into a paper cup.

"I'm going to visit an old art class of mine." She sips the black coffee. "Mmm, so good, this coffee takes me back to so many other cups of coffee I've had in my life, Myrna."

"Then you're time traveling."

Frances smiles, likes that idea.

On the upper deck, her mind rests in Rome at the *Campo de' Fiori* at a sidewalk café where she drank cappuccino each morning. There, she was a perfectly beautiful young woman—religious, a nun, wearing a habit of blue and white. Before she'd taken her solemn vows, she'd lived in Italy for three years where she completed a Master's in art history. She can almost smell the roasted coffee mingling with sweet faces of Botticelli's women, the graceful lines of Bernini's sculptures, and her love of art.

When a seagull swoops down toward her hand, she fumbles with the hot coffee, spilling it on her red coat. She becomes aware of the men and women around her on the ferry, hoping they haven't been watching her. Her eyes rest on a particular woman with a chiseled nose sitting across from her, talking on a cell phone, her head tilted peculiarly. The woman is beautiful enough to be a model for Botticelli's *Primavera* or one of the Sabine women in Bernini's *Rape of the Sabines*. She stares at the woman, unable to take her eyes off her; it's her pertness, her knowing look, her confidence. When the woman glares back, Frances bows her head, not wishing to intrude on her privacy.

When the boat docks in San Francisco, she heads for the disembarkation area, keeping pace, almost touching the tall Sabine woman with the chiseled nose who wears a stylish dark suit and Nikes. She can't take her eyes off her, reminded of her sister Anne. Lately she sees Anne everywhere, and yet in reality she hasn't seen her for fourteen years except in her dreams.

The younger woman stops and faces Frances. "Look, you're too close, and I don't like it. Quit following me. You're creeping me out!"

Frances drops her coffee cup; the black liquid spatters down her front. The wool sucks up what doesn't reach the concrete pavement. She stares at the small brown puddle.

The woman crosses the Embarcadero and disappears into the morning crowd. Frances knows that the woman with the chiseled nose will protect herself from being stolen away, unlike the poor Sabine women who were kidnapped in the early legends of Rome. At the traffic island she waits for a trolley to Fisherman's Wharf, wondering how she could have lost Anne in the way she did. She gets in the streetcar, rerunning in the mill of her mind the events leading up to her separation from her vocation and her sister, beginning with her expulsion from her Order.

2

The Expulsion from the Garden

On the day of her dismissal fifteen years ago, Sister Frances walked the long corridor of the Catholic university in her summer habit. The floors were slick and so highly polished that she could see her reflection. Standing tall, she walked one step ahead of the other in a straight line, vaguely aware of the occasional cross that hung on the walls beside her. A wing-like shaft of light cast a gray veil on the floor, perpendicular to her path. The shadow followed her like a great bird as her loafers tapped along the polished floor, leaving an echo. She stopped at Father Justin's doorway and put her ear against the solid wood, feeling its cool smoothness; smelling the resin of oak, she waited.

In this long moment outside his door, she remembered the day she'd first decided to open the small gospels. She was thirty-five years old, just home from Italy, new to the Order. She'd begun reading everything she could find as if she were

fitting pieces into a great puzzle. Like a detective, she'd comb
the library stacks to satisfy her curious mind until she came
to the shelves holding the sacred texts. She stopped in front
of the gospels whose bindings seemed to glow, calling her
attention. In fact, they were beaming light, though when she
looked around the stacks she saw the light in the room was
uniformly even. But the books still glowed, inviting her to
touch them, asking her to open them. She felt an uncomfortable heat rise in her body that made her leave the stacks,
yet she continued to visit the books daily as if they were
neighbors from a faraway land, asking to be included into
her kinship. She stared at their covers at first, not touching:
the translations of the *Nag Hammadi* Collection—*the Gospel
of Thomas,* the *Gospel of Philip,* and then the *Gospel of Mary
Magdalene.* They stared back, seeming to pull her closer to
visit them. She stood there repeating to herself, "Open or not,
open or not," reminding her of a game she'd play as a child.

"Am I meant to open the *Gospel of Mary Magdalene,*
dear Lord?", she asked, looking for a sign. The compelling
title drew her closer to the shelved book. Her heartbeat
drummed as heat rose in her body. She had to walk the aisles
again, away from the stacks and the vortex.

Finally, she stopped in front of the shelf and took the
book in hand. The book, surprisingly heavy, rested in her
hand like a warm stone. She opened the *Gospel of Mary.* First
she saw photographs of the text's original nine pages, frayed
at their edges, written in the peculiar Coptic language. She
faced the indecipherable picture-like words, each page written on small pieces of paper—eleven and one half by twelve
centimeters? The cuneiform pictures piqued her curiosity.
She imagined herself cracking a secret code. She thought of

how Carl Reinhardt must have felt when he stumbled upon the text in a Cairo market in 1896. She felt a kinship with him now over her discovery in the stacks of her library. Her heart throbbed as she thumbed the scant nine pages in Coptic and two smaller fragments in Greek. Here the gospel existed in translation for the world to read, yet she had never heard about it.

She opened the text to the dialogue between Mary, Peter, Andrew, and Levi. The dialogue flowed easily, and she could imagine herself being part of the small group of apostles gathered around Mary Magdalene waiting to hear His words. She looked for a chair, but finding none she slid down onto the floor and resumed reading the English translation. Mary was telling the others about the conversation she had had with the risen Christ. They called Mary "Sister"; they told her she was loved more than they were. They beseeched her to tell them what the Savior had taught her alone. She told them Christ's message of how the soul could find its final resting place.

This information turned Frances' head into a spiral; her stomach churned. She didn't want to hold this knowledge alone. Like fire, the little book burned in her hands. She imagined the stigmata reported by the saints. She closed the book, slid it back next to the others, and brushed her dark blue dress and her hair with her hands. Little fibers of cloth and her hair seemed to stand on end, electrified it seemed. She decided she would make a point to bring these manuscripts to her superior's attention as if it were her fate to bring the role of Mary Magdalene the Apostle out of the closet.

• • •

Now, ten years later, she faced the formidable wooden door, repeating to herself, *Knock or not, open or not, run or not?* She put her ear to the door and listened at Father Justin's private chambers. Not a sound. She could hear a catch in her throat as she swallowed. She knocked. The door opened and the tall thin priest wearing a black shirt and white collar stood there.

"Come in, Sister Frances," he said, stepping aside to allow her to pass through. He pointed to a chair in front of a long mahogany desk while he made his way to his own seat on the opposite side.

Frances focused on the delicate man with the tidy hands. Hands, white with perfectly trimmed nails, pulled at the arm rests of his seat to get in closer to the large desk. His orderliness provided form to this formless meeting he'd called. Frances stared at the long fingers before her as they slowly and meticulously opened a manila folder with her name typed neatly on the tab. The wear of the folder was in stark contrast to his hands. Each time she came to the office for review, there appeared another fold, another crease, another mark on the folder, like scars, reminding her of the wounds on Christ's body.

The priest opened the file and took out an evaluation which sat on top of what looked to be photographs. He read slowly, looking down all the time, unlike his usual manner of looking straight at her, boring into her soul.

"Sister Michael." She prickled and sat up tall, hearing him address her in her formal name. "We have a student complaint." He read, "*In recent lectures, Sister Michael presented material from the* Nag Hammadi *Collection—the Gospels of Thomas and Philip. And the Gospel of Mary Magdalene. These gospels suggest and reference Mary Magdalene's relationship with Jesus, suggesting an erotic connection. And more, they imply that she was His chief apostle, the one who knew intimately Jesus' teachings.*" Father Justin bore into her eyes now and then went on. "*Sister Michael has gone so far as to say that Mary Magdalene is an equal partner in the wisdom teachings of Christ.*" The priest looked up again into Frances' eyes, as if expecting something.

"Sister Michael."

"Father."

She looked into her teacher's eyes, the teacher who had willingly discussed with her for these ten years the role of Mary Magdalene in teaching the gospel. Why was he calling her on these writings now? She sat in disbelief, not knowing where to go from here.

She sighed deeply. "You yourself have lectured on the new findings in the gospels of Mary, Philip, and Thomas, Father." When he didn't respond, she continued. "We have acknowledged together and within our community that these gospels concur with the canonical gospels of Luke and John." He sat unmovable. She went on.

"Like the other gospels, they date back to the first half of the second century. That's all, Father. You would think we are still in antiquity by your reaction to this young student's complaints about my teachings. These findings exist yet they have been seriously suppressed."

"And you, Sister, must be the one to un-suppress them?" He raised his voice uncharacteristically and hunched forward toward her, exposing yellowed teeth.

She met his stare. "Yes, Father, because it is the truth. We, as women, must have a voice." His white hands flurried like bird wings as he resumed silence. "I mustn't have a will of my own. Is that it, Father? Is it the game of Mother May I?"

Father's face twisted, and he seemed to struggle to speak as if a chasm existed between his previous support of her work and this new and different stance. "Sister, I have stood by your excellent work, but now there is further evidence that calls for another action." He tapped his thin fingers on the photographic papers now sitting on the manila folder.

Frances remained in stillness staring at the priest who had indeed supported her in the past. Molasses minutes passed before he pulled out the other papers. "Is this your work, Sister?" He turned over the sheet and placed it in front of her on the desk. She stared at the photo of a painting of a voluptuous woman hanging from the cross, a Christ figure.

Frances sat up taller, eyes widened and mouth dropped open, as her hands trembled. A strong pulse sent a shock down her spine to her feet, making her shoes feel much smaller. Here were photographic images of original paintings she'd done in the basement of the convent where she lived in Rome in her mid-twenties, before taking her final vows. How is this possible? She wondered. She remembered removing the three canvases from their stretcher bars, rolling them into a carpet tube, and sending them to the United States to her grandfather's art dealer, thinking some day she would retrieve them. Had someone photographed them when they sat languishing in the convent basement in Rome?

"Sister Michael."

"Yes, Father." She waited sitting in silence, focusing on her rapid breathing and beating heart as if it could jump out of its sheath and shout at the betrayal she experienced. When she finally settled, she asked him where and how he had received photographs of her original art works.

He only responded by fingering the corner of the photographic paper, seeming to wait for her to explain herself.

"Father," she said, "I never wanted to share these paintings. They are my personal prayers, a sentiment between me and my creator."

"Nevertheless, they may be seen by the others as sacrilegious, irreverent."

"The others?" Frances looked to his downcast eyes, wondering who these others were and why he hadn't stood up for her as he'd done in the past. She wanted so much to know he would defend her, though the photo of her female's nudity on the cross begged otherwise.

"These works are both sacred and religious to me." Regaining her composure, she took the stance that Father Justin had once admired in her and continued to express her thoughts directly.

"Isn't the sacred both agonizing and joyful? Look at our dear Christ." She paused, waiting. When he did not respond, she tried another angle.

"This is what art is. It brings spirit and matter together to create wholeness. Like *conunctio* in our sacred readings, it brings together the dualities in a unitive way."

"Your painting is irreverent and erotic," he said, avoiding her eyes.

"Yes, it is. And art and creation are both erotic and irreverent . . . bring opposites together."

"God is the Creator, Sister, and not a man or a woman."

"Creative spirit is within you, Father Justin."

They each sat in their own quiet contemplation. She no longer felt the safety she once felt with her mentor. Sadness and hurt crept inside her from his betrayal. He looked limp and crestfallen as his hands fluttered and his mouth drooped. She wondered if he felt shame at the exposure of a female Christ or disappointment in Frances.

"Father, why?"

"I'm sorry, Frances," he said, kindly now, reverting to her given name. For a moment things felt as they always had. "But you will be dismissed nonetheless."

Deep down she believed he didn't want to dismiss her, but his hands were tied. He could not support her on this issue.

"You, of course, can expect a small severance from the university. I will see to that."

She stood up, but not before signing the resignation that sat among the pile of papers. "Thank you, Father."

●   ●   ●

Two weeks after her dismissal, Frances appeared, small valise in hand, at her sister Anne's doorstep in the Richmond District of San Francisco—the same place Frances had lived in her early teens with Anne and Mother after Daddy died. She waited in the small vestibule with a heavy heart and her few belongings, wishing she had told her Mother Superior the truth about her leaving, barely saying goodbye to the other nuns. She swallowed a lump of sadness.

The sound of the door opening brought Frances to the present moment. A young woman with intense black eyes stood staring at her, with her head tilted to the left, eyebrows raised into an unspoken question: Why'd you go and quit? Again.

"Anne," Frances said, "you still wear your hair short but the bangs are new."

Anne, thin and petite, had shiny black hair like the mane

of a baby colt. Her cheekbones high, her teeth white with a gap between the top two. She wore jeans and a white short-sleeve tee, exposing small tight muscles on her upper arms. Her developed musculature, results from early years of ballet training, only accented her flat chest.

"Frances," she said finally. "You let your hair grow. It's so red and wild. A wild strawberry color. You don't tint it? Do you? I thought . . . "

"Maybe you thought I'd be veiled. We did away with that with Pope John Paul." Frances paused to examine the modern young woman. "And yours, so stylish, isn't it?"

"I'm glad you phoned me. I've missed you."

"Thank you." Frances looked at her sister, brought her hand to her chest, and tapped three times.

"Let me take your bag," Anne said, reaching for the handles. But Frances didn't let go, so they squeezed through the door into the apartment, each holding one handle, walking side by side, their shoulders touching. Then Anne pulled harder from her side, loosening the bag from Frances' grip, and walked it into the hallway. It was like arm wrestling, where one tried to get the other's arm down on the table. Anne had won.

"You can stay here while you decide what to do. Does it feel weird to be living in the same house again?"

"A little," Frances said, looking down the long hallway to the far room, once their mother's room.

"You'll be staying in Mama's old bedroom." Anne walked into the living room. "Your old room is a small office now."

"Mama's old bedroom," Frances repeated. "I haven't been here in this house since Mama's funeral."

"Yeah, and that was sixteen years ago." Anne stood to face her. Frances rubbed her hands in circles on her own cheeks and then landed her extended fingers over her eyes, welcoming the absence of light.

"Where does time go?" Frances uncovered her eyes. "You're thirty-seven and still so beautiful. Do I see a silver thread in your hair?" Frances pecked her cheek the way she used to when Anne was a tyke. Her sister pulled away.

"Franny, I never understood why you left to go into the convent. And I don't really know why you've left now after twenty years. Are you ill? Exclaustration sounds like a disease."

"Time to reevaluate, that's all," she placed trembling fingers into her skirt pocket, turned away, remembering exactly why she'd left home. The invitation to join Sacred Heart School came at a time when her home life seemed to be crumbling. Considering a contemplative life of service, living with other young women while receiving a private school education appealed to her. So seductive was it, she barely gave a thought to leaving Anne and her mother or how that might have affected Anne.

"That's all, time to reevaluate?" Anne's voice rose, calling Frances to this moment.

Frances felt her heart rate increase the way it did when someone saw too closely into her—the way Anne just did. What could she possibly say in a few words?

"I'm leaving. Just that."

"No reason," Anne said.

"Freedom. Only thing I'll miss are the women. I hate leaving my community of friends."

"The way you hated leaving Mama and me?" Anne stamped her foot. "You ran out on us when Mama was sick. Why do you always leave, Franny?"

Frances grew silent. She wanted Anne to give it up, but

she pushed, standing intently with her hands on her hips, waiting, demanding an answer from Frances.

"It was bad timing . . . my leaving. I had to begin my vocation." Frances bit hard on her lower lip, thinking how she left the mess at home and now another mess at the university. She didn't tell her she'd been fired for being a renegade, that she had threatened the male authority.

Anne broke into her thoughts, "You always do what you want, Franny. You're selfish in that way."

"Yes," Frances managed to say, feeling the sting. She took Anne's hand in hers. "Can you ever forgive me for running out on you? My running away wasn't meant to hurt you, though it must seem that way."

"It's just so fast, Franny." Anne pulled her hand away. "You've got to give me some time. You can't just rush in here and expect me to forgive you."

Frances turned to leave. Then stopped herself. "I don't want to run out on you again, Anne."

"Oh, It's just all so mixed up for me." Anne looked at Frances, seeming to see through her.

Frances' legs shook like they wanted to inch out the door, but she stood there in front of Anne, whose face seemed to soften.

"Now I'm remembering how I could never hold anything against you for long, Franny. And you weren't always selfish with me." Frances sighed more easily, squeezing her hands together.

"Do you remember taking me to your favorite tree house and how we hid in there for hours? And the way Mama always made you take me along? A teenager with a six-year-old! Must have been hard on you. Let me put some tea on for us and we can sit and talk like civilized people." She went into the small kitchen and poured water into a stainless steel pot then turned toward Frances, motioning her to sit in the armchair in the living room. But Frances followed her into the kitchen.

"I was nine when Daddy died. Do you remember how I wouldn't talk," Anne said, "and how you saved me?"

"Did I?" Frances didn't remember. What she remembered was taking a leave from boarding school and coming home to help her mother and sister through those times. Vividly, she recalled the funeral and Anne, just nine years old, wearing white lacy ankle socks and patent leather shoes, impulsively hopping up into the casket to get her daddy to wake up, begging him to wake up. Frances' heart had pulled on her that day in the funeral parlor as her hands reached into the casket to pull Anne out and into her arms. Frances remembered Anne scraping her bare leg on the thorn of a rose and how the blood beaded on Frances' white woolen sweater.

"You miss him so much, don't you?" Frances said.

Anne hugged herself, curling herself tightly in at the mention of Daddy's death. Was it death and loss that frightened Anne so, or her belief that only Frances could save her? Frances was aware of deep threads of loss that lay hidden between them.

The afternoon light made a perfect triangle on Anne's sharp nose. Frances stared at the shadow on Anne's face as if the answer lay there. She wanted to hold her, the way she might a child, to tell her that death was the other side of life and not to be feared. But this would be smug foolery.

When Anne got herself together, she looked up at Frances with life returned to her eyes. "The guest room is ready.

Freshen up while I get the tea." She motioned Frances toward the foyer entry. Her voice rose, "You must be tired. You've been over the world and back."

From the foyer Frances looked at Anne in profile and felt a longing for her. She only half-knew her sister. Eons of time, days and weeks and months and years, had slipped away. Frances stared at Anne as she poured the hot water over the tea leaves, feeling frozen as if she'd lost her bearings.

•   •   •

Except for attending Anne and Greg's wedding ten years before, she hadn't really spent time with them. She didn't really know them as a couple except to see them under an arbor in the Golden Gate Park rose garden, taking their vows of marriage, holding hands while their eyes glistened as they repeated their homemade promises.

"I'm glad you're home now," Anne said, walking toward her with a tray holding two cups and a small pot of tea.

"I've missed so much of your life. I'm so sorry. And how is that man of yours?"

"He'll be happy to get to know you."

Frances looked at the shiny wooden floors in the spanking clean apartment. She kept house the way Mama did: you could eat off the floor.

"Mama would have loved to have seen you married." Frances thought it sad that their mama hadn't met him. Look how she kept house, married, and worked in a start-up company. Mama would have been proud of Anne.

"Mama would have loved Greg. You know how she always wanted me to marry," Anne said.

"She would have loved to have had grandbabies too." As soon as she said this she felt a pang in her heart. Neither of them had children, and Anne looked away. Frances wished she could take it back.

"Hey, I'm making your favorite dish tonight," Anne said. "Chicken *al rosemarino*, ravioli with pesto, and for dessert, Mama's *cassata*."

"You'll never get rid of me."

They laughed and then hugged. Frances could feel Anne's bones, like a sparrow. She quelled the urge to pick her up and rock her in her arms, the little bird of her life.

Frances looked around the living room, seeing family photos looming up from the mantle of the past. A gallery in folding metal frames peered back at Frances. Both sets of grandparents perched on either side of Mama and Daddy, ghosts from another world. Nonna Giuseppina and Pa Nicola sat elegantly in the den of the old beautiful house. Pa wore a thin mustache, dress clothes, and leather shoes, resting his painter's hand on Frances' shoulder. She sat by his feet while he held baby Anne on his lap.

The other set of grandparents, stiffly posed, looked uncomfortable in clothes that weren't reflective of who they were. Pa Antonio, the laborer, would have worn a flannel shirt, and Nonna Caterina a floral housedress, instead of this Sunday suit and dress. In the photo Anne and Frances sat on her generous lap, her soft flabby arms working their love around them. Frances could almost feel the succor of the protective cloak Nonna wove to hold them safely. The middle photo of Mama and Daddy is what pulled her away. They stood with the dog between them, noticeably without the children, Daddy's arm outstretched to pet Poker.

Frances' eyes flew to the Venetian glass vase on the mantle over the fireplace. "Oh, you have Mama's tiny vase," she said, taking the cobalt-blue fluted glass from the mantle into her hand, fingering its spiraled edges, smooth and sensual to the touch. Then she held it up to the light, watching the colors dance and shimmer. "Mama bought this on her one trip to Italy. I always loved it."

"And it's yours. She left that to you. I'm growing fond of it, though. If you don't take it this time, it's mine, though she meant it for you. Take it." Anne came closer and placed her hand on the vase lovingly. Frances held on, letting herself feel the warmth of Anne's skin next to her own.

Anne insisted she bring the blue vase to the guest room and settle in. Frances unpacked her few soft undershirts and panties, a half slip, three pairs of woolen socks, a soft cashmere sweater, a second tweed skirt, a white linen dress, three white hankies, and one crocheted hankie that was her Nonna's. Lastly, from her skirt pocket she took her pearl rosary, which was missing three beads from the ten sorrowful mysteries, and placed it under the pillow. The blue vase sat on the night table next to a pretty silk pouch belonging to Anne. They seemed to match.

The smells of the basil opened her senses, bringing joy and appetite, making her mouth water. It was just like Anne to use recipes from Mama and Nonna. At dinner Frances let the *basilico* sit on her tongue, tasting the flavors of garlic and pine nuts mixed with the *parmigiano* cheese and letting the texture of the smooth, soft ricotta-stuffed ravioli pillow melt on her tongue.

Anne, Greg, and Frances ate this first dinner together, chatting about work and family news until well after the sun went down. They laughed about how Nonna never seemed to mind their pinching her soft flabby underarms. Anne showed Greg the game, reaching over to pinch his biceps.

"This doesn't work, Greg. You have toned muscle here." She pinched again. He let her demonstrate on his arm, his long thin face and dark eyes opening into a smile.

"Didn't that Italian music and dancing bring out the witches and goblins?" Anne pulled on Frances' arm to show Greg how they danced in those early days, how she pinched the flab.

Greg listened and laughed with them. He'd just bought a Sony Walkman and passed the earphones around so they could hear Abba singing "Super Trooper." Where had she been? In another world, where *Agnus Dei* and *Ave Maria* reigned. After the wine they listened to The Police, "Don't Stand So Close to Me", a band new to Frances. "No, that won't do." Anne put on Nonna's favorite music, *La Tarantella*, and they all swung around arm in arm like they were at a country barn raising, doing the do-si-do.

Anne and Greg laughed together, poked at each other, and danced. Frances felt at ease in their company, enjoying the way they joked with each other like playmates. She couldn't help feeling a pang of envy, of yearning for such a bond with another. Frances wanted to show a happy face for them, which was not hard; their youthful chumminess charmed her. Where had her own youth gone? But was it her own youth she longed for? No, more her sister's. A missing link from the nine-year-old girl to the grown woman before her. She wanted Anne back; she missed her. She wanted the child to play with and to love. She choked back a gag in her throat. She didn't even know this woman laughing with Greg.

•   •   •

Anne spent most of her days at the small start-up company south of Market Street, while Frances walked and read, listening to birds that seemed to call her from her preoccupations. The fresh air and exercise cleared out the cobwebs. Starting over scared her. What would she do? What if she were blackballed from teaching as a lay teacher in any school? Would Father see fit to give her a reference? She considered modeling Anne's life, which seemed so new to Frances. What did she do? A start-up company, a husband? She didn't understand what Anne did, but wanted it.

Frances rode Anne's bicycle around the city, enjoying the physical sensation of her muscles working the pedals. Greg joined her on these bike rides when he had the afternoon off from work. He was a marketing consultant for California agriculture. Usually he wore his Walkman as they rode side by side, or he in the lead. When her stamina increased, they rode over the Golden Gate Bridge to Marin or along the Great Highway. He was her guide and seemed to love introducing her to new music and bike routes.

Whenever they stopped to rest, he'd plug one of her ears into the Sony and they'd listen together, standing side by side. The plethora of songs, songs she'd never heard before, excited her senses. As a new tune came on he named it for her, shouting, "Emotional Rescue," "Hungry Heart," "Ashes to Ashes." She would make up incredible stories for him about poignant titles he loved hearing, and they doubled over with laughter. Frances was glad there was no "Ave Maria" on his Hit Parade.

Their playfulness, though unexpected, was a gift after

the strain she'd experienced in her Order. Though ten years younger, Greg wanted to be her *inspiriteur*, her life coach. She'd never been around younger men in this way. The priests weren't playful, though they coached for sure.

One afternoon after bicycle riding to Sausalito and back, Frances was in the basement doing laundry. She heard the clanking sounds of Greg working in the front of the basement, rustling in his toolbox; she smelled the smoke of his cigarette.

Though focused on the clothes she pulled from the dryer, she pictured him in his spandex bike clothes, taking a drag on his cigarette. When he came up and stopped behind her, she smelled the peppermint Lifesaver he liked to chew after smoking. He lingered there, and when she bent to retrieve her clothes, he pressed his legs against hers, moving himself close to her buttocks. She felt the heat of his body through her skirt and then his warm breath on her neck, raising small bumps, the same sensation she'd felt dancing years ago with Elvis. Only there was no TV between her and Greg, just his soft breath, his warm body, and his minty smell.

She knew this was totally wrong; she knew that without question. It was not too late to move away, to push past him and head upstairs. But she didn't. She let herself indulge in the feel of his soft kisses on her neck, relishing this experience, letting herself melt into him like butter warming and then changing from solid to liquid. Though she had let herself become one with her Lord, she had never experienced this merging on a physical level.

When she turned slowly to look into his eyes, he pushed his face forward, close in, letting his lips touch her lips. They easily parted to allow his tongue to slip in, rolling and searching the warm womb of her mouth. He tasted of mint and the cigarette he'd just smoked.

Their hands fumbled and groped for each other as he unbuttoned the cardigan sweater she wore. He touched her erect nipples. Beginning in her deep center a great spiral began to grow, sending circles that rose and expanded, pulling her to elevations she had only ever experienced spiritually. Now she felt them physically, her body vibrating, each spiral changing color, reaching a climax that could not expand further, but must fly out. Soft like a bird opening her wings yet loud like sirens exploding, feelings she could not control.

Places deep inside her throbbed with a sensation that bordered on pain. He lifted her skirt and slipped into her panties. Their bodies convulsed in an erotic dance that culminated in a deep profusion of color. She moved closer toward him, her animal nature awakening her senses. Vibrating like a musical instrument, she wanted to be played. She stayed in his arms, taking him in, marveling at the clean smell of his semen.

Time went slowly before she settled down and could hear the hiss of the washer again. His heavy breathing had quieted. The sound of a car outside alerted her, but still she could not move away from him. Like a bird after hitting a glass window, her body wanted to sink into the ground. She supported herself on the washer, rubbing her fingers into the woolen skirt, pulling weave, clinging to loose threads in the material. He moved slightly. Sounds creaked in the old frame, alarming Frances. Every creak brought the possibility of Anne opening the garage door, and Frances dying of humiliation. How could she ever face her like this? She pulled a long strand of her hair until she felt the sting on her scalp. Disgusted by what she had let happen, yielding to temptation. Or worse still, had she been the temptress?

Sickness unto death, an existential prayer of Kierkegaard, took hold of her being.

"What have we done?" she asked Greg.

"We've just had sex," he said softly in a whisper. "Fran, is this the first time?"

"Yes," she said, the casual comment piquing her to the point of disgust, heightened by the acrid taste of his cigarette smoke rolling around in her mouth. He held her tightly. She pushed him away.

When he reached for her hand, she wanted to take him in again. She wanted to spit him out. They stared at each other. Silently Frances turned away and went upstairs. With feet prickly and numb and limbs rubbery, she grabbed onto the railing feeling dirty, soiled, no longer whole. She washed quickly and within half an hour, avoiding any encounter with Greg, she left the apartment with her few belongings, wrapping the blue fluted vase in her sweater and tucking it into her valise.

Her valise felt heavy. She meant to take only what was given, the vase, but was leaving with what was not given.

3

Mea Culpa

As the trolley car stops at Fisherman's Wharf, Frances wakes up from her memories of what happened and how she'd left Anne fourteen years ago, feeling remorse and a deep shame at her behavior. She walks briskly away from these feelings, inhaling deeply as if the air will cleanse her. She passes the Dolphin South End Club, Ghirardelli Square, Muni Pier, and climbs up the hill and down into Fort Mason, stopping at Greens' takeout for a second coffee and a scone, which she carries upstairs, stopping at the first landing to admire the view, the expanse of Marina Green leading to the Golden Gate Bridge on one side and Alcatraz on the other, with Sausalito just beyond. The abstract shapes of the scene below, the triangles of the suspension bridge, and the stone-cold line of Alcatraz meeting the sea bring a painting to mind, one she's done or has yet to do.

The cold metal steps, not unlike those on her own boat, comfort her as she opens the white waxy bag. Rough fingers trace the perimeter of the scone. "Triangular," she whispers, removing the gem from the bag. She first bites off one corner of the buttery dough with a crystalized sugar coating. Pecan and orange zest mix with her saliva, revealing a symphony of tastes. Then she bites off a second corner before sipping the still-hot coffee. Golden crumbs rest on her large bosom.

On the second landing, she opens the metal door and walks down a narrow hallway, passing the drying room where paintings rest in slots. She imagines them as lost souls separated from their creators. On her left she stops automatically in front of her former locker, number forty-nine. This art class had been her refuge when she left Anne and Greg in such a hurry fifteen years ago. She stands staring at locker forty-nine where she used to store oils, brushes, a gray woolen sweater that was her grandfather's, and a pair of old shoes. She even remembers 34-4-34, her combination.

Frozen in front of the orange metal storage bin, she sees herself as she was then: forty-five and pregnant, living with Sister Mary as a lay-person, dressed in a black woolen sweater and a tweed skirt with an expanding front panel that would accommodate her growing tummy over the months that followed.

The old tool box holds the palette knife, the hard edge, the screwdriver she'd use to open her gesso, small tubes of Windsor Newton paints, expensive *Sennelier* from money she'd eked out from her last paycheck from her position at the university. The tubes run together. The cadmiums—yellows and reds, light and medium—sit together; then the vermillion, the alizarin crimson rest next to the burnt and raw siennas. The third space holds the cooler colors—phthalo blue and green, cerulean, ultramarine and cobalt, and her favorite, indigo, a dark blue, almost black color.

She looks through the metal door with X-ray vision, seeing the well-worn brown T-strap shoes splattered with paint, the neatly folded gray woolen cardigan sweater that Papa Nicola used to wear on winter days when he'd let her mix the colors in his home studio.

Her heart fills as she recalls her old painter grandpa having done what she loves to do, teaching her how to mix paint with the right amounts of linseed oil and damar varnish with stand oil; how to lay her paints out in oppositions of orange against blue, red against green, yellow against purple. She crosses her arms, caressing her body, caressing the image of her papa, who'd been a mentor to Alan Sterling in Alan's early days at the Art Institute. Painting with Alan brought her closer to Papa Nicola; painting in this classroom with Alan was like being in her papa's studio in the old Belvedere house before he died, in his mid-fifties, of tuberculosis when she was nine. Mixed feelings of death and the excitement of creation invigorate her. She jiggles the lock. It doesn't open. Of course, it wouldn't. She hasn't been here for fourteen years.

She then moves to the far doorway of the art room and steps inside. The long rectangular room, with large industrial windows facing Greens' in the direction of the Marina and the Golden Gate Bridge, is exactly as she remembers it. She walks to the front of the large studio space and sees opposite the windows and between the two doors, the white walls smattered with assorted paint strokes of every color and pinpricks where her canvases had been pinned into the wall—canvases mural-size, sometimes six or seven feet wide.

Small tables and wooden easels stand helter-skelter; a platform used for models rests in the center. The yellow metal cabinets that contain lethal thinners, turpentine, and oil mediums are locked with a chain. Below the faucets, two deep and darkly soiled sinks wait. Frances can hear the water as it pours over soapy fingers, squishing paint from hairy brushes that have been soaked in solvent. She makes a full sweep of the room to make sure she is alone.

Before sitting down on one of the stools, she covers the seat with a piece of paper, knowing how paint has a way of finding clothing. As she smells the residues of thinners and oils, she closes her eyes and imagines seeing her former classmates file into the painting studio.

Mostly women artists, the women at the studio reminded her of the sisters in the convent in the way they coddled each other and had fun. When she first went to the school she'd imagined they wanted to touch her tummy and to feel the heart beat of the new life growing inside. Frances wanted to engage with them in a playful way, to celebrate this new life given to her, but she had to put a restraint on her joy. No matter she wanted their blessings. But how could she have shouted out her excitement at feeling life stir within her when it had cost her so much? Look what she had lost. Look what she had done. Not only had she abandoned Anne again, but worse, she had held inside her the baby Anne couldn't have. It was bittersweet.

Sitting in the classroom now, she wonders how she'd managed the early months of her pregnancy.

There was Cora, in her seventies and recently retired. "Frances, you better paint for two. My mother used to tell me to eat for two. I got as big as a house!"

"Don't you even listen to that one, you'll get as fat as she is," Elsa, the oldest among them, shouted.

Cruce laughed, poking Cora. "Eat for two, she's always kidding."

Frances wanted to hear these old tales, the chitchat, and to receive their wisdom to eat for two, but she couldn't indulge them so freely. But they didn't know. She couldn't blame them for not knowing how she stole this baby. She turned away toward Leah and Zel, Chrissie and Jane, Annie, Kathy, Jo, and Naomi, who were setting up their easels and palettes when Alan announced a current exhibit he'd seen at SFMOMA.

"Has anyone seen it? If not, you should see Manuel Neri's work. He paints large canvases of ghostlike figures. They are sculptural in quality."

"Isn't he a sculptor?"

"Competition for Giacometti."

"Have you seen the Arneson exhibit?"

Alan Sterling stood tall, a head over her shoulder as she painted in front of a six-by-five-foot canvas pinned to the wall.

"Keep going. Then do another one."

"Another one! But this is not finished!" she said.

"It's working. Do a half dozen more. Your gestural quality is your strength. And go see Neri at SFMOMA. Look at Odilon Redon, and Dufy, too," he recommended. "I think you'll like the Fauve artists, as well."

Wasn't Alan validating her creativity? She believed that through his encouragement of her work, he was honoring her pregnancy as well, because Frances believed that her success was related to the baby growing inside her. He was providing the inspiration. But she didn't tell Alan that her unborn child helped her to paint for two or twice as good. She didn't tell Alan how his support helped her feel deserving of this new life given to her by God. Her meaning pointed to creating beauty in the world. And that is what she would do—paint beauty in this world!

• • •

Opening her eyes now, Frances sees with absolute clarity how Alan saw her and understood her work. For him, her paintings were alive. He didn't see the grayness and blackness of her life in the habit she'd worn for so many years. The black and white was gone, replaced with colorful movements as if painted by whirling dervishes. No stoic nuns lined up in a row. And now he's dead.

She regrets that they had not been in touch these fourteen years and that she had not told him how much he mattered to her. She realizes she has exiled herself from all whom she loves. The sobering thought brings to mind the Madonna and Child series, which emerged in those early months of her pregnancy and reflected not only joyful anticipation of the birth of a child but sadness as well.

As she reflects on her work, she's aware of the despair she painted into the eyes of the Madonna. Deep fluid eyes downcast, with shadows of gray daring to cover her rosy cheeks. More like the eyes of the *Mater Dolorosa*, Lamenting Virgin, the virgin of tears and sorrow, than *Virgo Gaudens*, the joyful virgin. Mary held the infant Jesus close to her breast, but her eyes spoke of a sadness foretelling the loss of her only son. This recognition is stunning for Frances. Her loss was foretold, but she had missed the cues.

Frances bends her head away from the disturbing image only to find another one emerge—of a crying woman, the one who came to Frances when she lived with Sister Mary.

Mary was a renegade nun who had made her house a ministry for grieving women. Frances had just left Anne's house, not knowing she was pregnant, when Sister Mary asked Frances to help out by seeing this grieving woman. Perhaps Mary understood the workings of God by putting them together.

The woman was grieving for her toddler at the time. "We were celebrating at my brother's new house. Jimmie just started crawling. I set him down on the floor. We were toasting, and when I looked down, I didn't see my baby. He'd crawled away in a split second. We searched, running down the steps and toward the pond. When I looked over the railing I saw his green tank top floating on the top of the water. Belly down like he was looking for fish."

Frances, then three months pregnant, sat in front of the crying woman, who clung to the tiny striped cap her baby wore, letting her tears wash her face. She dabbed her eyes with the little cap. Frances thought the woman's confession to be inappropriate given her state, and yet imagined that it was her state that had elicited the confession in the first place. Frances didn't cry with the grieving mother, not letting herself too close to the horror of the death of a child. Instead a screen came down between her and the lamenting woman. In this vacant, cold art studio she cries with the poor woman. *Can you forgive me my sins? My aloofness? My coldness toward you?* Now she sobs for the woman, for herself, and for her dear sister whom she lost twice.

Frances gets up from the covered metal stool and starts moving frantically, swings her arms, sweeping figure eights and great arcs, dancing her feet toward the painting wall as if this movement will console her, will bring back the lost opportunities for more peaceful choices. All that remains are the ghosts of her loves. The ghost of Alan Sterling; the ghost of Grandfather Nicola; the ghost of Anne. The lost baby Jimmie of the grieving mother and her own lost child. All of them, ghosts, and yet together perhaps. Somewhere.

Why have I come here today? She remembers the reason: Alan's death. In her mind she sees herself as an old lady dancing and swinging her arms in the middle of an empty classroom, sniffing turpentine, waving her hands in the air. A lost soul hidden in a red coat walks where the teacher would have been, searching for those blue eyes that used to twinkle with sparks of joy, those thin lips that said, "Keep painting, Frances."

She flicks off the florescent lights and leaves the room. On the fire escape, she pauses briefly to look out at the bay, letting herself sit on the stairwell again, peering out at the cold blue gray water and Alcatraz, thinking only of solitary confinement, The Rock in the middle of the bay. *They were imprisoned for far less.* She prays, *Save me, Dear Papa, have mercy on me.*

Begin again today.

She yearns for *absolutio*, to be set free from her sin. Or is it *dissolutio* she wants, to be dissolved into a state of nothingness?

4

Surprise Visit

The ferry disembarks in the center of Sausalito where well-dressed tourists linger at gallery window displays and outdoor restaurants. Frances pushes through them toward the street beyond, the street where the locals hang out. She heads for a small restaurant no larger than the size of a one-car garage where she can hide. At the door, she peeks inside to see people in small groups of two and three chatting and eating at tables covered with floral oilcloth. The large splashes of blue, red, and yellow plastic floral designs lift up her heart and remind her of her childhood. Her mother liked cheesecloth colors. She walks in, past a lone man with papers neatly organized in front and around him who takes up a table for four for himself. She scurries past everyone toward the bathroom, down a short narrow hallway with closed doors on both sides.

The smells of toilet soap mix with cardamom and sautéed onions, making a true masala. She hides for a while, not ready to face anyone. She instead indulges in picturing the counter where the short woman with the orange pants will serve all the people who come, refusing no one. In the restroom she lingers, refreshing her face with cold water. She pulls back what seems like a mop of unruly hair. Her face, red with splotches, makes her feel sick. She leaves the bathroom slowly and walks toward the main room. But she stops short in the hallway between the freezer and the closed closets.

"My sister lives here. Her name is Frances Pia del Aqua. Do you know her?" comes a man's familiar voice.

"She lives in Sausalito?" Frances pictures Bimi's inquiring mind and serious warm face, taking her time.

"Sali, this man is looking for Frances." Frances gasps from the narrow hallway, holding her breath.

"She's not here today," comes the voice from the small kitchen behind the register. Frances pictures the cook bending out to see the inquirer.

"Your sister, Frances, the older woman with the gray hair? Older than you?" The woman says, "I didn't know she has brother."

"Yes, we don't see each other much."

"I didn't know she has family. You don't know where she lives?"

"She lives on a boat."

"What's your name? In case she comes here later?"

"My name is Greg. Greg Randall."

"Why you don't have the same name as your sister? Your sister's name, Frances Pia," she asks, raising her voice to a higher pitch.

"That's because she's not his sister," comes a third voice. Frances is surprised to see her friend Otto at the tea counter only yards away. She makes herself thin by squeezing up against the wall that leads to the restroom and a back exit. Otto has his back to her. He's walking toward Greg. Then the white-haired man stops. Frances imagines Otto's stare as they lock eyes. A cup of chai steams in his gnarly hands. Frances cranes her neck to see the two men facing each other. The eighty-something elder challenges Greg.

"I'm her brother. I haven't seen her in a couple of years."

"And what do you want with Frances Pia, young man?" Frances listens quietly to his Norwegian high pitch and peeks to see him walk closer to the glass counter with his wire-rimmed glasses in his free hand.

"Pardon me," Greg says.

"You are an impostor!"

"And who are you? Who the hell do you think you are, the Pope, some fucking do-gooder, policing the joint?"

"My name is Otto."

"Are you her mother confessor?" Greg shouts loud enough so that others in the café stir. She hears chairs scraping the floor.

"You might say that. She confides in me enough for me to know you're full of shit!"

A small crowd of customers gather around the two men. "Tell her I was asking for her."

"She'll know, she has friends here," Otto says, turning toward the people gathered around, who are shaking their heads in agreement with the older man.

"Screw you," Greg mumbles.

"You want another? Your turnover's crushed," the woman asks. Frances sees a bright saffron hand around the fried turnover.

He asks for a napkin to wipe his hands, pays her, and heads out of there, turning left past the Nori-ko Restaurant next door.

When Greg leaves, Frances sees Otto, who is surrounded by the other patrons in the café. She takes this opportunity to rush out the back door of the small restaurant, not wanting to see him or to have to explain who this person is. Gripped by an irrational fear that something terrible has happened to Anne, she trembles. A dread takes hold of her, making her want to run after Greg to have him allay her fear. But she feels dizzy and can't seem to run. Trembling, she sits down on the paved driveway behind the restaurant, waiting as images of the past flood her mind.

She'd made the decision to suck it up and go to Anne and Greg's house to introduce them to the three-month-old baby. She felt free and happy for the first time in months and ready to show them her baby. She remembers the floral skirt and cloth sack she wore around her shoulders and front to carry the infant, Nicola, named after her grandpa.

Nic was asleep and still and it might look to others that she was carrying fruits in her sack—round, ripe, precious fruits. She rang the bell and waited. Greg came down and at first only stared at Frances and her sack as if she were a peasant selling her wares. But the baby whimpered and moved so that little pink fists with curled fingers tucked inside of them came out of the sack then swiped the sides of his face and found his mouth. He began to suckle.

Greg was speechless. He stared at Frances and the baby. Then he turned away and closed the door on them.

•   •   •

"Frances, you're sitting on the cold pavement," Otto reaches out his hand to her.

"Oh, you've come for me, beloved Papa," she says. "How do you always know the right time to come and comfort me?"

Otto smiles and pulls her up. "Let us sit on the corner bench."

"I knew you'd come. I prayed you'd come to save me from these pictures I see today."

They walk silently, hand in hand, toward the lone wooden bench on the corner of the street and sit facing down the block ahead of them. Frances puts her hands on his face, convinced she's sitting with her dear old Papa.

Otto places his swollen hand on her knee and sits silently, waiting with her, letting this bench hold them. "Crying will wash away the cobwebs, get you to the next place," he gently urges. She nods.

"You saw him, didn't you, dear Papa. I prayed to you today to save me." She turns and looks into his old eyes. "Oh, it's you, Otto," she says, coming to. "I thought for a moment . . ."

"I saved you from your phony brother. How is it that he's not a bit like you?"

She doesn't want to talk. She wants to sit with him and enjoy how he protected her from Greg.

"He's my sister's husband. You scared him off, Otto."

"Why's he looking for you?"

"I don't know. Last I saw him, fourteen years ago, he turned his back on us. Shut us out of their lives."

"Us?"

"Me and my baby."

Otto takes her hand, brings it to his mouth and plants a soft kiss there.

"I wonder what he wants from me?" she asks aloud, but Otto doesn't answer. She continues, "He's been living away from me as if he's dead, as if I'm dead."

Again Frances feels alarmed that something might be wrong with Anne, and wonders if she should go after him. Why else would he show up after all these years? She gets up suddenly and leaves Otto with a quick bow and walks toward the bay, pulling her coat tightly to her chest, holding her breath and shivering at the chill wind. The fog is draping the hills to the west bringing cold air, which seems to blow from the wrong direction.

As she nears the pier, she spots Greg staring at the two small boats moored to the dock, not far from her own dinghy. What's he looking at? Does he know the one he's peering into belongs to her?

He turns, facing her. His stare penetrates.

She backs away. She has cold feet.

"Frances!" He's walking toward her.

Her head swings around, her blue eyes peer at him. He stops ten feet in front of her. Has he changed so much? He comes closer, stares. He's older, fuller. He hasn't shaved in days. Has she shrunk? Is she more bent, more ruddy, more wrinkled than the last time he saw her in his vestibule? He moves closer again. Face to face, they stare without words. Their eyes hold onto each other. Neither moves toward nor away.

"Hello, Frances." He breaks the lock.

Her shoulders rise, almost touching her ears. Then she asks, "Has something happened to Anne?"

"No, Anne is fine."

Frances relaxes. That is all she wants to know from him. "Then why are you here?"

"Your grandfather's work, a show."

Her eyebrows lift and her breath skips.

"Anne planned with Alan Sterling for a retrospective at the de Young in December. You knew?"

She did, but she didn't know Anne would be involved.

"Does she want me there?"

Greg shifts from foot to foot.

"She doesn't." The thought reverberates in an echo chamber in her being. Anne doesn't want her there. She doesn't want her there. Frances had left her before and again. And now Anne doesn't want her there. The days without her would extend to the depths of time. Frances yearns for the taste of her *rosemarino* chicken, for the eucalyptus smell of her sister.

"I heard you live anchor-out, a renter of space on the bay."

"No rent. I'm an unauthorized live-aboard."

"Is that why you live out there rather than on the docks?"

"The unauthorized part or the rent-free?" she asks, then says, "Look, the boat was a gift. I don't want to make small talk with you. What do you want after all these years, Greg, to talk about property rights?"

"Frances, I want to see the child."

"Don't, Greg," she pulls away instinctively. "You made your choice. You closed the door in our faces." Frances wipes her calloused hand across her reddened cheek, feeling the prickle of roughness sting, and walks away from the pier in the direction of a café, determined to get him away from her boat which is tied only twenty feet away. He follows.

"Where's the boy now?"

As if she hasn't heard him, she walks faster up the incline, slightly ahead of him. He follows a step behind her.

When they get to the sidewalk near Café Trieste he's keeping pace with her.

"Did you tell Anne about our visit, about the boy?"

"Why did you come to our house that day?"

"I wanted you both to know of his existence. For you to meet him."

"That's crazy shit, Frances. What about Anne's feelings? Did you even think of her?"

"Anne can manage her own feelings. And you, your own."

"Some things are better kept hidden," Greg says.

"And yet now you want to meet him?"

"I do. Can we sit and talk a minute?" He looks toward the only free table in the crowded café.

She nods.

While he gets the table, she stands at the crowded bar, comforted by the line of people in front and behind her who wait to order coffees and watch the *espresso* machine grind the dark powder. Waiting to order gives her time to collect herself and figure out what she'll say. She feels the pulse of his needs, the urgency beats like hard rain. Something dark like a storm cloud is building up inside, ripening and threatening to burst. To divert these feelings, she mouths the words that move across the silent TV screen above the bar, empty words announcing a silenced football game.

She looks toward where he's sitting, focusing on his shiny leather shoes that look like they hurt his feet. These clothes are too formal for out here, but he doesn't know any better. He doesn't fit in here. Greg is looking at his wristwatch now, bouncing his leg. His agitation is palpable, yet he sits silently with his knuckles cemented on the table, looking from his watch to the line of people. The weight of his quiet restlessness enters into her like dark grinds of the espresso melting into the waiting cup.

Frances looks toward the barista and orders a black tea, takes her order number, and sits down, resigned to hear him out, resigned to tell him.

"Why now?" she asks, playing with the number twenty-seven. "What makes you want to know now, after all these years?"

She feels the vibration from his bouncing leg.

"To set it straight. No that's not exactly it. I want to know about the boy. Can you tell me, please?"

"The boy," she says, as a pot of tea with a mesh strainer arrives. The waiter places an empty cup near the steeping pot and takes the number back to the counter. She stirs the empty cup with a teaspoon.

His other leg begins bouncing beneath the table, rumbling the pot.

"I wish when you showed up that day with that pouch around you I could have been different. I couldn't grasp that I made you pregnant. You left so quickly, you never came back, Frances, until—"

"—a year later," she finishes his sentence. "But even you could have deduced that he was yours. Sex makes a baby, Greg. A fact older than man."

He looks down into her eyes as her voice raises a notch. She snaps as if she's breaking open something solidified in an ice chamber.

"And Anne? Does she know that sex makes babies or doesn't she have sex with you anymore?"

Greg recoils, clutching his sides.

"She doesn't know you came to the house that day. She doesn't even know you have a child. I didn't tell her."

"Does she know why I left so quickly then? At least she knows we had sex? You at least told her that, right?" She taps the tea strainer on the ridge of the cup, splashing tea leaves.

"She knows that."

"But the rest . . ." Frances' mouth falls open. "She doesn't know you're a father."

"No."

It seems like a sin to her that Anne doesn't know of her child's existence. Her skin erupts in hives and she looks down to watch them break out, one by one. Pink and then pinker. The irritation reminds her of her mortal sin that cannot be blotted out.

"I'm sorry."

"That's an old song, Greg. You can do better than that!" She looks around to the patrons at the nearby tables, assessing their interest in her conversation, realizing her voice is bounding out loud. She stops and bites her chafed lips as if that will slow her down.

"Anyway . . . here's a new lyric for your song, Greg. Brace yourself. There's no boy. He's dead." She imagines everyone jeering, chiding her deed. She whispers, "The boy is dead."

She doesn't move.

A cold silence envelops them, freezing them to the seat. Are they encased in a frozen landscape where time stops? Then a shiver of sadness washes over her as if she's lost her best friend. Her vertebrae, like the Russian stacking dolls, seem to sink one into the next, cracking like ice crystal.

She sees her child as a one year old on the day he died, on the day her heart congealed into an ice cube, leaving her frigid and cold. Nicola, in his blue knitted sweater and cap, sat in the infant bicycle seat, secured by a belt as she pedaled over hills to the park swings. She heard him laughing as she pedaled, wanting so much to turn around to see the way his eyes glowed when he laughed; she wanted to squeeze his little fat cheeks. She couldn't take her eyes off him. *Why can't someone invent a bike seat that faces forward on the bars so parents can see their babies' faces?* As she sang to him, "You are My Sunshine," he cooed. Oh how he loved to swing in the park, and she wanted to give him that pleasure; she pedaled harder. It tickled her to see him laughing out loud. To be truthful, she wanted her own joyous feelings that he inspired.

Nicola laughed and babbled, catching his little breath, exhilarated by the slight downhill. She could see his bright face in her mind's eye. The day was young, and the birds twittered in the magnolia tree. White and pink flowers bloomed.

"Look up there, Nic, at the birdies."

Nic pointed and said, "Beer, see." He was beginning to put two words together.

Before they entered the park they played in the grass, inspecting the fallen blossoms from the tree next door. His small fingers could pick up the magnolia petal between his thumb and pointer, delicately holding it in the air for the birdie to see. He held onto the flower as they entered the park.

She doesn't notice the band has set up on the small stage in the café; a woman is playing a sax; a keyboard player is singing; Russell has entered the café and is moving toward them. She only feels a salty wetness slide down her craggy lined face and into her mouth. Ravines chiseled by tears erode her skin, leaving deep crevices in red clay. She sits like a mountain of stone in her great sorrow.

A woman is singing, "Baby It's Cold Outside."

Her body shakes. Goosebumps rise on her flesh.

Greg stops. Frances stops. How long they sit there or how many songs go by, she doesn't know.

"Frances."

She looks at him.

He reaches out for her hand.

She turns her face. She cannot tell him what she's never told anyone before. She can't tell him what a bad mother she was.

"I'm sorry. Can you ever forgive . . . " Greg asks.

She watches as his fingers nervously tip the tea strainer. The wet tea leaves clump on the table. Her longing for Anne sets in. It's old, and its weight is heavy. Her shoulders sag.

"Is she still mad at me?" Frances asks.

"She doesn't speak of you."

"She doesn't speak of me?"

He nods.

"I ran away from her, from you. I wish I'd come back every day until she knew the truth, until she answered the door."

Greg excuses himself to go to the bathroom. She knows then that he is just like her, a runner. But what's worse is that she let him steal what was most important—her relationship to Anne.

When he returns, Frances is sitting with Russell at a different table, directly in front of the jazz band. Wearing a sailor's cap and a soft fleece, he has his arm on her chair, leaning his thin face into hers, following the wet crease of her cheek with his index finger. Greg stops in front of them. Russell only has eyes for Frances. Frances sits in silence.

"Well, I think I'll be getting back to San Francisco and let you two . . ." Greg lingers, seeming to want something more from Frances.

"Goodbye, Greg," she says, not making eye contact.

"I want to hear more about the boy. I'll be back."

Russell stands up. "You best be going."

5

Cormorants

Hundreds of cormorants settle by her boat, a carpet of black velvet. She watches them as they skim the surface of the water before lifting into flight. Black shimmering beings rush all at the same time, urged by some mysterious signal, swooping past her as she stands at the stern of her boat. The whir of their wings roars as they lift off, flying low at first with their slow metronome call. Then they circle her boat and those of her neighbors in frenzied and dizzying directions, creating a spiral of black, not unlike a mini tornado. All the while the anchored boats point toward the northwest, glowing in early pink light. Then, standing in the silence of the birds' absence, she faces Russell's anchor.

"That's why we're alive!" yells Russell, who stands at the stern of his boat as well. His voice startles her. She reaches instinctively for the line to her dinghy to make sure it's attached safely around the cleat.

"What a spectacle! From another world. Spirits, aren't they?" she says softly. After last night with Greg, she's grateful to be back on her boat, grateful for the natural part of her life; but Greg said he'd be back. The thought crowds in now. Would she confess to him what she's never told anyone?

She opens the storage bin and pulls out her wetsuit, surveying the water. No wind. The water in the bay is glass, slate green-black, begging her to enter.

"You going in?" Russell asks, motioning with his hands back and forth from the water to her, a kind of Morse code they sometimes use.

"Yeah." As fine a day as any to shock her nerves after her sins of yesterday. She knows she stabbed Greg with her news, but worse, she was mean-spirited about it. In a few moments, she'll make amends when the frigid Pacific water stabs, cuts into her and then soothes every pore.

Every time she jumps into the icy bay reminds her of the moment when the child breathed his last breath, because the frigid water takes her breath away too. That single moment is indelibly marked on her soul with ink *noir*. She sees baby Nic laughing and then flying away like the whir of the cormorants.

She leans onto the gunwale and talks to Nic as if he were beside her. *Nicola, you were so happy in that swing, kicking your feet so hard that your right shoe flipped off.*

I didn't know I'd put you in the wrong swing. I didn't know Nicola. Can you forgive me?

Feeling the splintering wood of the peeling gunwale pressing into her butt, she recalls his laughter, which brings enough joy to fill the sea. Then she begins to choke on this unearned mirth, coughing hysterically. She reaches toward her neck, smoothing down the loose flesh as the familiar fear grabs and tightens itself around her throat. She struggles with an invisible rope that seems to wrap itself twice around her neck. Pulling at her collar, she gasps for air, panting, trying desperately to catch her breath. She wrestles as a demon takes hold.

"God! Damn! Stop it! Let me loose!" she shouts before she's in the grip of another coughing spasm. She wrestles the invisible hold until she lies flat on her back in the cockpit. It's not the boy doing this to her. It's Him, her Lord God, on whom she's turned her back.

Exhausted by all the thrashing on the floor of her boat, she places her hand over her racing heart. *What is happening to me? Did I not ask You forgiveness? Our Father, forgive me my trespasses as I forgive others. Have I still something to learn with all this suffering? Must I be left defenseless?*

Frances pulls the wetsuit up over her hips and breasts, squeezing in her arms, then zipping up the back. When suited up with her boots and hat, she sits on the railing of her boat and flips over backward. The first rush of cold water oozes in between her suit and skin, momentarily paralyzing. Is this what she longs for? Is this numbness or is it aliveness? She loses her bearings, floating in some free unknowable state, suspended. A momentary freedom from her usual shackle, the black water pulls her at its will. Murky and deep, it seems to swallow her in its open mouth. She lets the water consume her.

The current moves into the bay and pushes her afield from her destination, the Spinnaker Restaurant and the ferry dock, less than a quarter mile swim that she does weekly. In a slack tide the round trip takes less than an hour. But, of course, she's going against the tide. She lets herself be pushed away from her goal, wanting momentarily to be swallowed up and set free. She forgets her destination—the small rocky beach on the other side of the restaurant.

As the current pulls her toward the rocks at Belvedere Point, it carries a single thought, one that Frances has never before considered: *If only I could sink.* Having always been enraptured by the surface of the sea, its colors of greens and blues with a vast sky above it, she has never contemplated the bottom, not to mention sinking.

If only I could sink, comes the clear wish. She finishes the sentence: *I would be free.* The Belvedere rocks sit stoically as the waves crash over them. She can see the shiny tendrils of kelp among stringy wet grasses, clinging to the rocks as the water pushes them frantically. The current's taking her dangerously close to the monoliths or, worse, out into Raccoon Strait, which is known for its whirlpools of currents as the tide pushes in and out of the narrows. She gulps water, fearing she will be swept away.

Holding her breath she delves into a swell, where sounds dull. *If I could only sink,* comes the now-familiar refrain, but her wet suit is too buoyant and so she bobs on top, where choppy whitecaps float on the ultramarine. Surely the weight she carries—the dead boy, the lost sister, Greg's visit, and her betrayal of God—is enough to sink her to the bottom.

She imagines the coastline of the bay as a great container for a deep pool of whirling water, with a bottom which holds the mysteries of the sea. She pictures a whalebone, a sunken ship, broken glass polished by time, rusted buoys, and chains like her own. The sound of water whooshes through her ears. It whispers, lulling her, rocking her in its great womb. She lets herself be held as a beautiful mermaid with the kelp hair, a female of both worlds. If she could sink, she would be in another world, where sound would be muted and dulled, and light would disappear. All would be quiet.

Is it the numbness in her nose, her icy fingers, or the flight of the cormorants lifting off from the rocky promontory that wakes her up? Sweeping closer, they almost touch her. Their shiny black wings, their whir so intense, send an energy that makes her think she can lift off alongside them. She looks toward the channel and the Spinnaker, and begins her swim against the current. She will not sink to the bottom today.

Now that she's come to, the same current that took her adrift provides resistance to her strokes. She pushes against the surge with every ounce of strength. Each inhalation and exhalation deepens as she nears the restaurant. She swims under the Spinnaker and out the other side, toward the rocky point on the far side of the restaurant. Then she swims toward the ferry landing. With no ferry coming in, she can be out of its way and make the round trip circuit easily and without stopping.

Swimming back with the current of incoming tide, she rides the blackish waters of this sea cradle, taking her back as easily as it took her away. How so? As she nears her boat, she sees Russell, suited up, in the water surveying his craft. She must have been in the water an hour. She swims up to him and grabs the line. Their eyes are linked by the watery mist. Two babes at sea.

"What will I do when he comes back?"

Russell dives under his boat, swimming toward the submerged anchor while Frances still clings to his ladder, looking toward her buoy with its rusty chain. Then she climbs up the ladder and into his boat, comforted knowing he's underneath. The black rubbery seal skin she wears heats her up, attracting the sun's rays, as she waits for Russell to reemerge from down below. Hot air circles between her skin and the suit as Russell circles beneath and around her worlds. She doesn't want him to know of her other life, of her sins.

When his head finally pops out of the water, she doesn't engage him about Greg's visit. Her voice feels limp. *Dear Lord,* she prays, *please show me another way so I don't drown this man with this nasty business, so that I don't suck the life out of him. Please help me.*

"Hey, Russell, maybe you could check the status of my anchor while you're in the water. Would you mind?" she says instead.

"Franny, we already know she's hanging on by a thread."

"The anchor or me?"

"That one," he says, looking toward the round red buoy bobbing that attaches to the anchor. "I don't trust her alone or the chain either. You don't want to be out there predawn, moving toward the rocks, dodging your neighbors."

"You mean hitting on you," she teases him as he hops up the ladder onto the deck. She reaches out to give him a hand then rubs his fingers from their frost. They stand silently, two seals in their skins, before he moves his hand.

"Like I said, living out here is not for the faint hearted."

"That's me."

"I don't buy it, Franny." He pinches her cheek.

She tilts her head, swooping her face toward him, brushing his cheek ever so slightly.

"You blushing, or is it that ruddy look I love?"

"I'm glowing in your presence." She winks and then moves to the rail and flips off the side, swimming back to her boat, surprised by the feathery tickle under her wet suit.

Gloria! She prays. *Deo laudamus te, benedicimus te, adoramus te.* Lord we praise and adore You. The Latin prayer she hasn't let herself pray in more than a decade rolls freely from her heart and out of her mouth like a song just waiting for this moment.

6

The Woman in Stone

The gentle roll in her berth nudges her awake. She doesn't open her eyes but focuses on the warmth from the golden light on her face. *Am I still alive?* she wonders, half-expecting to hear a bark from her mammal friends. Even the sea lions sleep this new day.

She looks through the porthole of her boat toward the eastern sky, with its first rays of deep cadmium yellow wrapped around a bright white core. This orb seems to nest in a vast black sea. A central golden ribbon divides the sea vertically, casting a copper cornucopia. On the horizon line, a thin band of tangerine traverses the darkness. Tangerine gives way to aquamarine, then white. Such a spectacle, this band of light, but the white looks too perfect to her, reminding her of God.

Is it You? Are You here to show me?

Then she imagines she is sixteen-year-old Frances, her mother threatening to jump out the kitchen window.

"Damn it, Frances, you won't go."

Mama was adamant about her staying home to take care of her sister so she could get to work at five. She was proud of her new job as a saleswoman in a classy dress shop, the new job she had gotten after Daddy died.

"But, Mom, it's only 2:30," Frances pleaded. "I'll be home in time."

"You're lying to me, Frances."

"Mom!"

"Don't Mom me. You're seeing that slut friend of yours."

"Maria is not a slut. That's disgusting."

"I hear the way you whisper about boys. You're disgusting. Don't think I don't know what you're up to!"

"I'm going. And without Anne."

That's when Mama opened the window in the pink-tiled kitchen and sat on the ledge, the way she did when she washed the outside of the windows. She hefted her foot up over the sill and sat there straddling it as if riding a horse. If Daddy were alive, he would have scolded her. Frances could hear him saying, "Get in, Gloria, that's three stories down. Quit your antics." But he wasn't there to chide her, so she sat perched like a pouting bird. One shoeless foot rested on the gold-speckled white linoleum floor while the other dangled outside. Frances imagined Mrs. Gertrude Klein, the old German lady who watched over the neighborhood, seeing this odd leg hanging out the window and calling the police.

Frances lowered her head to cover the icky feelings in her stomach, but all she could see was her mother's one calf with coarse hairs that grew like a man's beard; the opened housecoat exposed her thighs.

"I can't take this anymore. You better stop, you little shit, or I'll jump," she threatened. How could Frances predict what she'd do? She wanted to say, "Get in, Gloria," but she couldn't, so she backed off, putting her concerns and demands away. What Frances needed was for her mother to put her foot back into the kitchen and pick up her cigarette again. Leaving her mother on the window ledge, she turned and walked to the laundry room, picked up her book bag, and left the house.

•   •   •

Frances tosses in her bunk on her boat feeling her heart race as dread creeps in, fearful that the rage will escape and beat her to death. She rubs her face, taps her head, hoping to get rid of this kind of thinking. Her soft cheeks are like a baby's— warm and smooth and hot. She imagines them red. She looks toward the magnificent changing sky and tells herself to allow this moment and what it brings, knowing in her heart that it holds the good and the bad, the heavy heart, the heat, as well as the soft glorious light and the warmth of the rage on her skin. She obeys. As she lies there and the sky lightens, she allows the rest of that day to unfold in her memory.

She hadn't gone back in the house after her mother's threat or to the field to see the boys. Instead she'd gone to the Catholic Church of the Sacred Heart, entered through the side door, walked down the left aisle, and slipped into a pew, kneeling down on the hard knee rest. Above the altar, the suffering Christ hung without shame and in full view for all to see. He was practically naked and wore a crown of thorns with nails pierced through his hands and feet. His knees were bruised as well. She looked, wondering at the image, flashing briefly on the nakedness of her own mother hanging on the windowsill, her one leg dangling. One image superimposed over the other. Christ and her mother. Her mother and Christ.

Crucified.

Frances covered her eyes and looked again. Her mother's face, smeared with lipstick, was juxtaposed with His painted face. Both faces forlorn and brilliant at the same time, they hung together in her mind's gallery. His knees bruised and her mother's legs hairy.

The morning light throws geometric shapes of yellow onto the hull. She squints and rubs her eyes against the blinding awareness that her mother and Jesus are one and the same, that they both suffered, that she suffers, and that this suffering is the destiny of all humankind. The thought confuses her: even her mother, with her infantile needs, suffered.

Our Lady of perpetual help, pray for me.

•　　•　　•

That day sitting in the church she let solitude fill her. She sat listening to the quiet which swooped from the high ceiling, through the transom, and into her soul like a bird, filling her heart, giving her space to breathe. She sat absorbed by stillness until she heard the creek of the old wooden screen and then the whispers of a man and a woman. So near to the rectangular curtained booths, she could hear the priest talking through a screen window that opened to a small chamber where the parishioner made confession. Frances could make out the words of the woman confessing.

"Bless me Father for I have sinned. I have stolen from my brother . . ."

Frances kneeled hard on the wooden knee rest, driving her knees into the wood to distract herself from listening, knowing eavesdropping was a sin, too. "Father, he's mean to me and I hate him." She heard the priest whispering and praying with the woman. Then the woman left the booth, holding her hands over her face.

Frances, with her head up, knew at this moment that she too hated. Somehow naming her feeling freed her. When the woman left, Frances flew into the other side of the confessional. The priest was still praying. She didn't know what exactly she would say to him today. She had never really confessed deeply before, only recounting venial sins that allowed charity to exist, things like not taking out the garbage or telling white lies. No, that wasn't why she was here.

Then she heard the screen pull back and saw the shadow of Father Donovan, the priest who had confirmed her. She hoped he didn't remember who she was. She sat still, not moving an inch of her body. When he said she could take her time, she thought about what had just happened in the kitchen and then how the images of the crucified Christ mingled with her mother straddled on the windowsill.

"Bless me, Father, for I have sinned. My last confession was three weeks ago." He waited, she could hear his breath rising and falling. She counted three inhalations and three exhalations before she said, "I hate my mother." He waited. "Today I had the thought of pushing her out the window."

Expecting the worst, she waited behind the screen, but instead she heard a gentle voice. She imagined him smiling for her relief in telling him this secret.

"Take some time, dear child, and pray to the Virgin Mary. She will hold you in a safe and loving way." Frances felt relieved by his words.

"You are special to come here to confess," he said. "We often have urges, but you have done something different with yours. Say three Hail Mary's, an Our Father, and one Act of Contrition with me."

They prayed together softly. She imagined the great Mother Mary and Father Donovan holding her in a way that calmed and eased her, parents who wanted her to thrive. Erasing the suffering Christ from her mind, she replaced it with the gift of the dyad—Mary and the priest—and left the confessional feeling better prepared to do her job, whatever that would be.

•　•　•

Sitting on her bunk in the golden light, she knows that was the day she made her decision to become a nun. "Is this what You want me to see, dear Lord?" she asks now. The golden glow of the sun with the white center disappears, expanding to light the eastern sky. A bowl of roses spills from the clouds onto the sea and Angel Island emerges from the blackness. Russell's boat, a minute ago a dot of warm light, is silhouetted against Angel Island, a distinctly black shape, with its mast rising up into the growing azure.

At this first light, she throws on her shoes and readies her inflatable by pulling the line so that the boat edges to the stern, then places her bag under the seat. Carefully she lowers herself down the ladder and into the boat, unties and grips the oars. They glide through the sleek water, bringing her in on a smooth swell of calm water. Beneath the rubber of the inflatable is low tide. The shallow bottom stares at her but gives her room.

When she nears the dock, she sees a woman in the distance standing on the jetty. Familiar, yet strange. Is it the way she holds her head at a tilt or the way she hugs herself at the waist? She steps from side to side, a kind of jig you do when you're cold. Frances watches and waits before drawing her oars into the boat to meet the dock. When the woman sees Frances, she freezes in place. A stone woman. Then she's intent to get Frances' attention and quickly rushes toward her boat, now landing at the public pier.

A predator staring, what business does she have with me?

Frances looks behind her, thinking another boat is docking in the space there. But no, she's alone in her boat at the dock. There's only the lapping sounds of the water around her and the vibrations of this other's footsteps moving in on her. Frances clings to her raw woolen jacket against the wet fog that seems impervious to the rising sun on the opposite horizon. Squinting, she can make out more clearly the younger woman standing in front of her who wraps her arms around herself and tilts her head, holding still in the same cross-armed posture against the chill.

It's Anne.

Anne stares at Frances. Frances holds onto the cleat on the dock with one hand and touches her head making the sign of the cross, feeling the Army-Navy scarf she'd wrapped into a turban, a crown of thorns. Then she places both hands on the dock, hoists herself up, and slides her hips over the gunwale and onto the edge of the pier. One bent knee at a time, she climbs out, aware that Anne peers at her old bones.

Then Anne extends one hand in front of her as if she'd like to help an old woman up, but stops herself. Frances stands up tall, licks her lips, wipes the front of her coat as she walks toward Anne.

"Anne!"

Frances reaches her and touches the brown woolen jacket on her slender shoulder. Anne still feels to Frances like a little bird. Anne's face is pallid and her eyes are drawn with dark circles around them that culminate in soft white pillows beneath them. Anne looks into her face and places her hand on the craggy line that runs from her eye along the crease near her nose to her chapped lips. Frances bends her head down as a tear runs down this gully.

"Frances, you live in the bay. You're so old." Frances can only shake her head and emit a harrumph sound.

"You found me."

"Greg told me he came to see you yesterday. I needed to come. I can't believe . . ." she stops herself and withdraws, then says, "you live at sea."

"At sea, yes."

Anne stares at Frances then out at the water, a quizzical look on her face.

"How could you?"

Frances looks down, her chin seeming to slip inside her collar.

"I left him." Anne hugs herself and continues. "He told me last night about the baby, his baby. How could we live a big lie like that for so long, Franny?" Anne looks into her eyes.

"He never told you."

"Why didn't you come and find me and tell me yourself, Frances? Why did you disappear on me? Again. I called all your connections, Sister Mary, and no one knew. You disappeared from the face of the earth like Houdini. I thought you were dead." Her voice soars high, almost a scream. When her muscles soften, she says, "I'm leaving for India tomorrow. I've come to say goodbye. I suppose I need to get away to do some soul searching—to escape."

"Not escape, Anne. A journey," Frances says. "I'm the one who escapes."

They stare at each other; locked together.

Anne places a soft paper envelope in her hands. "Please read this," she says, then turns away into the fog spilling into the gap.

"Go in peace."

7

The Scaffold

Frances lingers, watching Anne disappear into the mist, pinching her hands, wondering if she's in a dream, if she's received a vision like Bernadette's. She walks away from the public pier as if on air, as if the world were right side up and whistling. She passes the docks where sailboats still sleep in their designated slips. Halyards clang on tall masts, ringing in her ears as she approaches her locker, one of the public storage units where she keeps her belongings safe from the eyes of wandering pirates.

She holds Anne's thin face in mind, sees the sad puffy eyes and wishes she could have held her face lovingly in her hands. She unlocks her footlocker and removes a small moveable cart, which holds a few belongings, then grabs the padded box with the small blue glass vase she took from Anne so long ago. Reaching inside, she takes the vase from the box and holds it up to the light, marveling at the swirl of blues that appear to be moving, molten yet still, like the sea. Holding the vessel close to her ear, she listens deeply and hears another heartbeat. The beating sound reminds her of baby Nicola's heartbeat. She takes the vessel to her heart and rocks from side to side, remembering the way she loved to cuddle him so close to her body.

She dips her finger inside, then brings fine powdered ashes of her baby up to her lips, tastes them, lets them rest on her tongue. They taste of a sweet dryness as they dissolve. Cast in what seems like a holy ritual, she makes the sign of the cross, remembering that today Catholics pray for all those souls in Purgatory. But surely her boy and other innocents are purified, she prays.

"Please, dear Lord, don't punish Nicola in Purgatory for my sins. And please watch over Anne, who needs your blessings." She focuses on the cart which holds the essentials of her life: a small bag with her toiletries, a thin plastic ground cloth, the long red woolen coat with the pearl rosary beads stuffed in a glove in the right pocket, a woolen skirt and sweater, and her towel.

Pushing the cart toward the public restrooms, she stops to look across the Bay toward Tiburon and Belvedere Point where she grew up. She can almost see Anne with her joyful innocence playing in the yard. Then Frances continues along the wharf toward the opening in the bay, focusing on the ashes still under her nails, wanting to believe the trembling in her hands is from the vibrations of the wheels that resist the coarse wooden planks, and not Anne's visit or thoughts of Purgatory. The wheels turn in on themselves, wriggle, and then go on course again. Death on her mind, a usual companion: death for herself, fear for Anne's death, Nic's death.

A natural and integral part of the life cycle, isn't it? Yet when she showed up at Anne's apartment and Anne seemed so sad about their daddy's death, Frances was so smug, so arrogant, to dismiss Anne's grief, she thinks now.

Rickety, clickety, rickety, dickity.

The sound mesmerizes her. The vibrations of the metal wheels on the roughly hewn boards of the pier shoot up through her feet, sending a tingling sensation into her palms. As the wheels bump along, she counts six hundred forty-eight boards, each attached to the one before it with one-inch bolts. Knowing the number grounds her, like saying the rosary with its five sets of ten beads each separated by the larger father bead. She looks over the railing to see the low tide. The water beneath the pier would be less than a foot deep. Grateful she didn't get hung up on a sandbar this morning, which would have made her miss Anne.

Passing door number one of the series of storage units on the pier tells her that there are forty-seven more planks to cross before she reaches the parking lot and a concrete surface, a civilized world where the wheels run smoothly. She parks the cart at the public restroom and heads for her favorite stall, the biggest one at the end of the row where Frances washes daily. Two face cloths, one with soap and another with rinse water. Invigorated, she dries herself with a small towel and dresses, then replaces her bra, which holds a small silk pocket she sewed in as a lining. Inside is a tiny relic bone from Nicola. She thinks it's his ear bone and that makes her happy. Sliding into a tweed woolen skirt and a soft black cardigan sweater gives her completeness, a kind of uniform that suggests status, she thinks. She places the pearl prayer beads in the skirt pocket. They slither along her fingers like a cold snake.

Then she combs through her long thick hair, fastening it with a red elastic band. She rubs a drop of olive oil on her face, promising she'll buy some real face cream with her next Social Security check that comes on the third Tuesday, general delivery. How frugal she's learned to be. Pride clings to her, making her feel virtuous for never having touched the money she inherited from her grandfather, which grows in a Bank of America savings account.

Frances sits on the park bench. Nearby, in the dried pine needles, pigeons scratch and itch as they peck for food. She focuses on one bird, all puffed up with her feet tucked under, neck folded in. She stares. They both sit so very still beneath the pine. High clouds and wind accompany the ferry into the dock. The sun, a full circle, is high on the horizon now.

Thank You for bringing Anne to me today, dear Father in heaven. May You forgive me my trespasses against my dearly beloved sister, and may this day be shown clearly to me through Your grace.

Walking past the restaurants, she smells the early morning fire from Poggio's wood-burning ovens. A delivery truck leaves replacement wood. Clothiers open and refresh merchandise. Officer Margaret Bentley walks her beat and greets Frances with a warm smile. Russell passes by on his bike, "Get the extra anchor, Franny." She doesn't know if he's asking or telling, but she keeps walking, dizzied by the beautiful gift of this day. Anne's presence is still with her, like a new warm light in her empty heart. Like the oven in the restaurant, she's being filled.

On Turney Street, Frances stops to watch a man painting a house. He wears a short-sleeve T-shirt that shows off his dark smooth skin. Music from a Mexican radio station blares as he paints, perched about ten feet from the ground on an elevated

platform. She watches him brush an arc of color across the face
of the newly prepped house. Her mouth falls open as she stares
at him, fascinated by his sweeping gestures as he applies the
paint. Or is it the Naples Yellow that stuns her?

As he works, he sways to the music from a small por-
table music box that rests on the scaffold near his feet. The
sounds from the ghetto blaster, which drips with yellow flags
of paint, seem to fly into her body, causing her to shift her
weight from side to side. With her hips gently rotating to the
beat, she watches him sweep the bit of sun across the face of
the gray wall of the Turney Street house, his head and neck
bobbing up and down, forward and back to the music.

Frances rushes toward the scaffold, stepping on the
crate, and hoists herself up, all in a split second. She stands
beside him, shadowing his movements. Anyone passing by
might think they were engaged in an erotic dance. An old
woman shadowing a younger man dancing on a stage. She
chuckles, thinking about her dear Jesus. What if Christ and
the two beside Him were dancing instead of hanging life-
lessly from that cross? She laughs at the image but reminds
herself she's here today to paint.

When the young man bends to dip his brush in the paint,
he notices her next to him. His mouth falls open, his dark eyes
widen. "Lady, what are you doing up here? How'd you—"

"Do you need help painting today?" She cuts him off
mid sentence.

"What?" he shouts, getting so close to her that she
steps back.

"I want to paint," she says, licking her lips. When he
stares at her with a confused look, she adds, "I want to work
with you today. You know, *trabajar*."

"You can't paint in that red coat," he tells her, shaking his head in disbelief and looking into her eyes as if he might better make out what's happening to him. He waves his paintbrush at her, gesturing for her to leave the way she came. She ignores him.

"Well, I'll take it off then," she answers, beginning to pull out of a sleeve.

"*Señora*, you can't work with me. It's dangerous up here."

She takes her coat off, neatly folding it, and then placing it near the radio. "I'm ready. Don't worry," she says, "I used to climb up the masts of sailboats over there." Frances looks over her shoulder toward the Tiburon side of Richardson Bay, where she makes out the tip of the island near the rock.

"You have to get down now," he demands. She ignores him, grabbing his brush instead, which he holds tightly. They tussle for a minute, tottering on the edge of the wooden planks until the brush falls, landing on the satin lining of the coat. The yellow paint mixing with the red of the lining creates a flaming image. They stare at it. Then he bends over to stop the music.

"Hey, young man, you can't turn off that music." She stamps her foot.

"You almost knocked me to the ground," he says, pulling his phone from his pocket, not taking his eyes off her as he makes a call. She hears him talking rapidly."*Una Señora, vieja, si, si . . . esta aqui. Venga.*"

And then he says some words that sound to her like a fast song. She only understands a few words but knows he's calling his boss, knows that she has disturbed his work.

As he speaks into the cell, Frances snatches a clean brush anyway. She feels an urgency rise up inside her, a familiar sensation that arises when something that matters to her will suddenly be taken away. She must get into the paint before it's too late. It feels as though her life depends on it. When she dips the four-inch brush into the yellow bucket, she becomes mesmerized. She watches the bristles enter into the vat of luscious paint, each one clinging onto the liquid color while the paint itself clings onto each hairy surface. The paint and the brush become one. She loves this feeling.

"And the music, *Señor*, please turn it on again," she says, oblivious to anything else but her pleasure. "Is that KGO?"

He ignores her, looking over his shoulder toward the street, swiping his smoothly shaven face beaded with sweat and stepping from one foot to the other, expectantly.

She paints a crisp line with the fine edge of her brush. The yellow glides smoothly across the gray wall like a ray of sun dancing onto the side of the house. The small stretch of yellow grows from a patch of sunlight into a golden field of wheat, abstract fields and open space. She remembers the subdued ochres her grandfather used in his large abstract murals.

A child again, she's watching her papa paint in his studio, mixing colors to make his soft yellows, showing her how to use the mediums, teaching her the secret formulas from the Old Masters—one part damar varnish, one part linseed stand oil, and five parts English turpentine. She can almost smell the solvent, which feeds her soul. Painting with the color and the medium is a relationship Frances can trust and one way to connect with her beloved grandpa.

Frances smacks her lips when she hears the young man say again, "*Señora*, get down." She ignores him, keeps painting, not wanting to leave her papa's side, so close is her memory; she can smell his woolen clothes that carry the smells of solvents, varnishes, and oils.

"*Señora.*" He gently touches her shoulder. "Umm, Mrs. I'm not the boss here. I could get in trouble. You're old. It's dangerous up here. You could fall and break a bone. Insurance and accidents—a big problem. The *jefe* will kill me!"

"I'll talk to your boss. Don't worry. It's not the first time I've been on an elevated platform. I live on a boat," Frances says. "Isn't it every man's right to be on a scaffold?"

The man frowns. "*Señora*, it's your age and you're a woman. You're as old as my *abuela*. My *jefe* would never let *Abuela* up here on these planks to paint a house in windy Sausalito."

"But I'm not your *abuela*, I'm Frances Margaret Pia, and I live out on a thirty-foot sailboat in Richardson Bay. I'm not your average gramma." She watches him shift from foot to foot.

"What does she do?" she asks. He looks puzzled. "Your *abuela*? What kind of work?"

"She works in the fields in *Ciudad, Señora.* She's a field hand. She harvests strawberries."

"Then she's no slouch. She loves color, too, like you. If she picks strawberries, then her red has a little blue in it. Doesn't it? I bet if she lived in Sausalito, she'd be here helping you, too. At least she'd know how to mix the colors like I do. Family, that's important," Frances says, turning toward him. "Tell me your name, son, and your *abuela*'s name?"

"Her name is Mercedia Maria Domingo Santa Cruz and I am Hernando Iglesio Santa Cruz."

"*Con mucho gusto*, Hernando. Now, let's get busy so you can go home before the sun sets today. And put up the music, *por favor.*"

"*Señora*, tell me something. Are you a bag lady?"

Frances doubles over in laughter. "You might say that. I

live out there in Sausalito Bay on a boat. I live anchor out, a bag lady at sea, I guess."

"You do?" stopping his movement, eyeing her, his head slightly askew. "How do you get to your boat?"

"Well, I don't swim. I row, what do you think?"

"I think that's unusual. You live out there alone?"

"Yes, except for the seals and the wild life." She doesn't tell him about the nightmares she frequently dreams; the lethargy that grips her, keeping her from doing the things she loves; the torpor holding her hostage; or how she has lost her family.

"Do you dream, Hernando?" she asks.

"Me, *Señora*? I dream of my home and my son in *la ciudad*."

"*Ciudad* Juarez?"

He laughs. "No I live in *Ciudad* San Rafael. I moved to California when I was ten years old. My brother is the *jefe*."

"If your brother is the jefe, he wouldn't fire you!"

"No, but he'll kill me if you break something."

A pickup truck stops below them. A slightly older man in his thirties gets out and walks toward them, wearing a pale blue shirt and jeans. Designer jeans, she thinks. He stops, and they all look at each other.

"*Buenas*, Nando. *Que pasa?*"

Hernando and the man speak rapidly. Though she can't catch the meaning, she catches Hernando's brother pointing a big finger at Hernando and then at her, back and forth, again and again. His hands are dark and big, sticking out of a soft blue cotton shirt. They look strong and competent enough to do just about anything. His right foot is shaking, like he has a restless leg. Frances feels horrible for causing them this trouble and for the way the *jefe* is yelling at Hernando.

What a wretch am I to have endangered his job and his boss's license.

She shifts her body, not wanting him to see her shame, which she imagines spills from her mouth and nose like green snot. She feels frantic inside, watched, like she's standing naked on the scaffold. What if she had done it differently? She might have been able to paint with him without jeopardizing his job. But even so, she knows she's compelled.

Bless me, Father, for I do sin, she prays.

"*Señora,*" she hears the man call to her. He hoists himself like a leopard up onto the platform, takes her arm, and escorts her toward the crate step below the scaffold.

"Let's get down now. Careful, please." She reluctantly follows, shimmies down with a jump at the end, but not before snatching a small can of semi-gloss.

"Perfect for the public restroom," she says softly.

Hernando sees her take the paint. He hands her the coat and says, "Take this too. You'll need a brush."

"*Gracias,*" she answers. Looking into his deep brown eyes she sees Nicola's bright eyes smiling at her. "I hope we can paint again under friendlier terms."

As Frances walks on toward the café, she fingers the soft hairs of the brush that Hernando put in her hands. Hernando, unlike her, is gentle and kind. She believes Nicola, whose ashes she touched so lovingly this morning, is blessing her today by bringing her close to the painter man who has an *abuela.*

The newly acquired yellow freckles on her hands seem to her like a gift, too. The late morning sun drenches her skin, suggesting to her the rainbows she wants to paint. She reaches inside her pocket for the unopened pint of semi-gloss that she's taken, running her fingers around the can, poking them into the groove, already anxious for her next job. Next to the can, she feels the unopened letter she received this morning from Anne, a silky onionskin paper, light. Her fingers press it, taking its pulse. It feels hot, like the manuscripts of Mary Magdalene felt. She squeezes the paper in her fingers and continues her walk toward the café.

At the café she sits down and orders a breakfast panini as a wave of despair replaces her manic glee, plunging her into her usual dark dance with God. "Thy will be done," she says, knowing He will have His will with her. The yellow sunny feeling dissolves.

Please dear Lord forgive me my sins; forgive me for all I have done intentionally or unintentionally to hurt Anne. I have caused her much grief, dismissed her. I know. Can You forgive my oblivious ways, how self-absorbed I am? May I not flee from You again. May I accept Your love, so that I may serve You and others.

She prays, rubbing her hands together. Then looks up.

Where are You and why don't You answer me? I hate Your silence.

The red she sees in her palm startles her.

She doesn't know she's been picking at the calloused spots on her palms until a small scab opens and a spot of blood oozes out. She watches the way the spot pools into a tiny puddle then grows into a small pond in the cup of her hand. She rubs her fingers in the puddle and then spreads it around her palm, wanting nothing more than to feel pain for her own sins.

The puddle begins to dry, changing to maroon, transforming into a dry crimson lake. She senses she is drying up, moving away from fluid youth toward her own cold dry death. She struggles to feel her feet on the ground beneath her chair; she pushes them into the concrete sidewalk, digging to the center; she sits on the edge of the wooden chair, so that she feels the gravity pulling her down; she touches the silky letter which seems to pulse through the pocket.

"This would be a good day for a glass of wine. No?" She opens her eyes to see Umberto, the waiter at her table, holding a panini and a glass of wine, or maybe it's a breakfast bellini.

Accepting the offering, she presses the glass on her lips, sipping the bubbliness of the drink. Raising her cup in kinship to those sitting at tables nearby, she salutes, letting the coolness effervesce through her, content at being part of this community. For a moment she has come back as a woman like others, who drinks and enjoys her food. She pauses. *Thank You for the food we are about to receive. May I be worthy of Your love. And please forgive the way I intruded into Hernando's space and stole the can of paint.*

She picks up the sandwich and bites the pink prosciutto, chewing the salty flesh, remembering the letter in her pocket. She pulls it out, places it carefully on the table, and watches it as she swallows. Finally she opens the letter and reads.

> *Franny,*
> *I must see you with my own eyes.*
>> *Oh, I know something awful happened between you and Greg, but you had a baby and I didn't even know. How could you keep this from me? I searched high and low, even looked out back up into the Eucalyptus tree.*
>> *Remember how you used to climb that tree with me on your back?*

It's been a roller coaster ride for me these years. I'm enraged at you and him one minute and then so sad that I lost you again. Mostly, I grieved your absence from my life. Grief is like a big wave that comes and goes with high peaks and low troughs.

Sometimes I remember what happened and that gnawing toothy conflict bites at my insides. I hope I can find you tomorrow before I leave for India. It may be the last time and I want to tell you I love you. I'm not sure I forgive you, but I love you, if that makes any sense.

Your sister,
Anne

Frances rereads the line about Anne's grief over and over, low troughs and high peaks, focusing on whether Anne can ever forgive her. Her face screws up in some bizarre mask.

The waiter is standing near the table staring. She turns her face into her collar.

"I can't even eat," she says. "The dear Lord is calling." She stands up, gathering her stuff together, and leaves to pay her bill at the counter. She heads toward the public restrooms with the small can of yellow paint she swiped from Hernando. A voice inside says, *Frances, no swiping! Frances, no swiping!* Frances quells the admonishing voice by telling herself that she's doing a public service; that stealth is sometimes needed, even rewarded; and, besides, Hernando was okay with it. She runs her fingers along the smooth edge of the bristles and walks without counting the planks on the boardwalk, pulled by her job to paint the public restroom.

The odor of antiseptic solvent greets her. *No one. Empty*

stalls. The tourists have left. Her favorite stall awaits her; the
sun casts a violet hue to the walls. She sets up a painting station, carefully resting the small can of yellow on the toilet
seat. *A can on the can,* she laughs. With ease, she uses a quarter to flip open the lid and then paints the inside of the door.
The yellow balances with the existing background color, creating a tension of opposites—violet shadows on yellow. Marveling at the peaceful aesthetic she's created gives purpose to
today. She hopes others will sense it, if not directly, sublimi-
nally. She cleans up, leaving a tag, 'Wet Paint!' on the outside
of the door. *Why not give something back to Sausalito?*

Outside, a small group of tourists disembark the late
ferry and walk past her. An old man, the centerpiece between
a teenaged boy and an old woman, has his arms on each of
their shoulders. Frances looks down at her tennis-shoed feet,
envying the man with the family. She might have had his
place with Nicola on one arm. Tears blur her vision, recalling
those years she spent without the boy, never seeing him as
child, a teenager. Then she misses her years in the convent
within a circle of women. They were so sweet, uncomplicated
in some ways.

*Oh, how alone I feel. Frances, let go. Let go. Allow. Time
for you to move on. Anne is moving on. Stop complaining
about your lot.*

I didn't know him as a boy, as a teenager. Oh, God!
she repeats.

She can't stifle her tears, wiping her snot on her sleeve,
the long white mucous reflecting the light. As self-pity
grips her, she gathers her stuff and with jittery limbs walks
toward her storage place before reaching her inflatable tied
up at the public pier. She wonders if she has the strength

needed to push the water, to make the dinghy move across the channel.

I thank You, God, for this simple home, anchor out. Please watch over me, I know not what I do.

8

A Ghost

"Your art, Franny?" Russell points to the long white roll as he pulls up to her stern. Frances carefully holds a forty-eight-inch artist's tube in one hand and looks toward her scroll, nodding. "It's a sketch of a nativity scene I'm working on for the Council Competition."

"You're not still religious, are you?"

"Not really. But I do believe that we, you and me, have a direct link to the divine."

"I don't know what that means, Franny."

"It means you see wholeness when you look at the bay, Russell."

"Well, it's simple then." He takes her free hand and helps her into his rowboat.

"It sure is. Simpler than getting into this boat."

They plan to shop for her anchor later in the day.

As they sit, they listen to the hum of his motor on the bay's glass surface. Frances closes her eyes and tilts her head up, letting the sun wash her face. The engine softens as Russell dims the motor and stops. When she turns, she sees the cormorants lifting off the water at the bow. Their magnificent blue-black shine rises, a dark cloud, with a whirring song that sends chills up her spine. They sit quietly, savoring a majestic moment.

"Can't put the motor on after that now, can we, Franny?"

"Can't now." She stares at his face, loving how the light casts a reddish glow on his bushy eyebrows and mustache that are uplifted to the sun. The hairs are soft and wild.

Russell gently swivels the oars on their locks and dips into the glassy dark water. The launch rises and falls gracefully forward and across the channel, like a sea mammal.

"You could get a girl used to taking a ride with you every morning, Russell," she teases.

"Could that girl be you, Franny?"

"It sure could. I like the slow sway of your moves." She winks at him.

They glide toward the public pier, with lapping sounds kissing the undersides of the boat. When Russell tucks in his oars for the final glide into the dock, Frances sees Greg on the public pier twenty feet away. She closes her eyes tightly, hoping to get rid of him, hoping she was mistaken.

He stands tall with his hands hidden in his windbreaker's pockets, waiting. She imagines his leg bouncing. It's all wrong; this man appearing in this glorious moment. Jittery, she leans forward in the boat to see him better. She feels faint, flexes her muscles, loses her balance, and falls over into Russell's arms.

"Franny, you're white as a sheet. What's out there?"

"A ghost, Russell, that's all." She hides her face in the nook of the long muscle of his neck, imagining its curve, its strength.

"Hey, Frances, I need to talk with you," Greg yells, standing beside the docking boat.

She clenches her body tighter to Russell. He intervenes, getting himself onto the dock between Greg and Frances. "What do you want from her?" Russell asks.

"I want to see her."

"Does it look like she's eager to see you?" Russell presses. He looks toward Frances and reaches a hand to help her onto the dock.

"Frances, I want to hear . . . about the boy, how he died."

She positions herself behind Russell as he lifts her up onto the dock. Greg pushes himself in between them and says again, "Please tell me where he is. How did he die?"

She touches her breast, patting it before looking directly into his eyes. "I told you he's dead. I killed him. Now get out of here."

Like a streak of wind, she pulls ahead and rushes across the landing toward the street. Greg rushes after her, yelling, "Frances, stop! Tell me what happened."

She hurries to the crosswalk, pressing the pedestrian signal on the pole. Without waiting, she dashes off the curb into the street against the red light. Greg rushes after, grabbing her upper arm just in time as a car slams on its brakes.

Still holding her arm, Greg apologizes. "I'm sorry, Frances. Can you forgive me?"

Frances looks at him, his anguished mouth twisted into a clown face, and for the first time, she feels for him. How has this happened, that she is rushing toward the place where Nic died with Greg following? She resigns herself to revisit the deed with him beside her as a witness.

"Follow me."

They walk in silence across Bridgeway and up Turney, stopping at a small park adjacent to the newly-painted yellow house that Hernando was working on. The park, a long narrow plot of land, has rough wooden chips as a ground covering. It is in disrepair; the city has been lax. It's used more for dogs and vagrants than children, it seems.

A dark pine tree shades the space. A jagged rock juts out of the earth near the tree. She shivers passing before it as they enter through a small gate. They walk toward a jungle gym and a swing set. Frances stops in front of one of three swings, the one that has a black belt at waist level. The waistband is slashed. Children can no longer be protected by it though they might be able to sit or stand on the seat part. The chains that hold it are rusty. Only the wooden frame structure of the swing seems intact.

She stands there, looking at the swing, her face drawn tight, her eyes held up as if by some invisible string, her breath stopped. Greg is next to her, waiting for some time, holding his breath, his hands held tightly in fists. When she catches her breath, he does as well. They seem to exhale together. Her eyes fall back down, her cheeks relax, her mouth is soft and open in a circle. Her hands fall limply by her sides. She feels like a child. Then she points to the middle of the structure, its ratty-looking swing.

"Here, he fell out here." She pushes the chain and the shabby swing swivels.

Greg looks at the dilapidated piece of equipment and then to the soiled ground beneath it, strewn with dried chips, occasional dog poop, cigarette butts, some urine smells. "So it's not your fault," he says.

She touches the now defunct swing where the cross

strap is cut. She wishes it had been so clear on that day. The rusty chains scrape her arm. She shakes her head at the city's negligence.

"I pushed too hard; he flew out and hit his head on a rock. There." She points at the jagged rock that looks like a piece of granite popping out of a cut tree trunk. A rough salt and pepper rock with a pointed top that little kids like to climb.

"Where?" He looks in front of the structure where she walks. He doesn't seem to see the small rock.

She kneels in the redwood chips about eight feet away from the middle swing. "Here," she points to the rock, half buried with its top sticking up less than a foot up from the ground, like the tip of an iceberg. How small it seems to her now, but then, thirteen years ago, it seemed like Everest with its deadly peak.

Greg walks toward the place where she's kneeling as she runs her fingers through the earth, clawing and stripping the dirt from the sides of the rock, digging to get to the bottom of it. She picks up a handful of earth stuff, rubs her hands together, and then massages the dirt into her moist cheeks. "Earth to earth, dust to dust," she whispers. She looks at Greg's face, his eyes sunken, staring at her. He seems like a babe in the woods. She doesn't know what he feels.

"Come kneel with me, Greg."

"You gotta be kidding, Frances."

"No, it's the right thing to do. I think kneeling down in this patch of dirt will give you what you asked for." Frances reaches her hand up toward his in invitation to kneel with her. Briefly she sees what might be fear in his expression.

He wriggles from foot to foot, takes his trembling hands from his pockets, and then obeys and falls down on his knees.

Hand in hand, they remain silent. It occurs to her that many suns and moons warmed and cooled the place; that the rains of thirteen winters watered it; that trillions of stars sprinkled their dust upon it. Yet it's as if the child passed today.

She prays, "Hail Mary, Mother of God, you who have also lost your only son, please bless this holy place and give me a sign." She repeats this prayer several times as if she were making a novena. As she prays beside him, she feels him sink deeper into the soil and sees his head fall forward, while his fingers begin to twitch. The spasm seems to climb to his hands and on up toward his lower arms as if shaking the earth. That's when she faces him and places her rough-ened fingers on his shoulders, pressing down into the earth, then she slides her hands down his arms; small they seem as she massages them. She smells his cigarette mint breath, oddly familiar.

When he quiets, she makes the sign of the cross on her forehead, remembering how her grandfather comforted her in this way. He'd tell her this was the only way to chase away the spell of an evil eye. She whispers some prayers, not really believing in the evil eye. Then touches him ever so lightly between his delicate brows, making a blessing for him too. She hears a gushing of sobs. Are they his or hers? She doesn't know. She reaches out to hold his hands. He gives them easily and sobs deeply, letting his tears water the place. With her warm words, she blesses him, *"In nomine patri et fili spiritus sancti."*

"You were alone, Frances, that day," he says, coming to, opening his eyes.

"No, I had Him, the one I always turn to in my sorrow. "

"Him?"

"Almighty God."

"How did you manage? Did you pick him up? Was his heart still beating? Did he die instantly?" He looks at her.

Frances fumbles with words. "It went too fast."

She feels numb—that feeling of badness collars her. She had pushed too hard, too high. She saw the twelve-month-old—one second laughing, eyes gleaming, and then flying, his head hitting the stone that killed him. Then puff! A light went out.

"It's not your fault, Frances. It was an accident."

"Thank you, Greg. I had Nic for a split second. He came out for a while and then he went back. Maybe he wasn't meant to stay. I carry him here always." She touches her heart again, reaching inside her blouse to pull out the tiny purse.

"I envy you the little you had him. I never . . ."

"You never did, Greg."

"Perhaps if I had been there, he would be alive today."

"Let's not to go back to what life could have been."

"I never touched him and that makes me sick."

"You never did. It's all wrong, except the fact of him." She opens the little purse and pulls out the tiny piece of white bone, shiny and smooth, and places it in Greg's hand. She watches a tear drop land in his palm. They stare at it, glistening there next to the bone, a fleck of white gold and a sliver of bone cupped in his thin tanned hand.

She listens to his sobs then he curls his hand around the little bone. He allows his fingers to cup it.

"God wants you to have this," Frances says. The silence grows as they sit by the rock.

She looks above a shade tree in the garden playground toward the sky. "I begged Him," she says, "but God remained silent. Sometimes I think He wants me to see something from this. But though I've searched, I find nothing at all. I think I am being punished."

"For what?"

"For what we did." She looks into his eyes.

"What we did was beautiful, too," he says.

She looks down. "He was the most precious gift of my life; he was beautiful."

"Anne's left me."

"I know. You still love her?"

"I do. I don't deserve her."

"Let's pray together." She takes his hands in hers. "Hail Mary, full of grace, the Lord is with thee. Blessed art thou among women and blessed is the fruit of thy womb, Jesus. Please protect our dear Anne, may she be safe." Then she adds a personal note to Anne. "I'm sorry for stealing the light from you, my beloved sister. I betrayed you, the first love of my heart."

After some moments, she gets up by bending on all fours. She lifts herself off the ground, brushes herself off, and helps Greg to his feet.

"Let's walk around the park and bless the ground here before we part." They begin walking slowly, first around the swing which seems to swivel as they near it, then around the embedded rock with the pointy spire where Nic met his fate.

Frances stops at the tree and says, "I can almost see him. Up in the tree smiling. I think he sees us." She smiles.

"I'll think about today and what you've given me," Greg says.

She looks over her shoulder toward him and then continues toward the water.

"May I walk with you back to the pier?" She nods. They walk together quietly. She thinks she can hear his heart beat.

Near the jetty, her face lights up to see Russell waiting there by his boat. He has not left the spot since her outburst about killing the child. Greg hands her off to him as if he is the father giving away the bride. Russell accepts her, puts his roughened hand on hers, fingering her fleshy palm. Russell and Greg stare into each other's eyes momentarily before Greg leaves and walks toward the street. Russell turns toward Frances.

When she sits on the dock, Russell sits near. Then he puts his hand gently on her shoulder and lets her head rest in the crook of his neck. They don't move, their breath in one body rising and falling together. Then, in one graceful swoop, Russell envelops her body next to his, so they are standing face to face, eyes smiling, fitting one into the other, breathing with each other as the sea breathes with them.

9

Splintering Wood

It's noontime a week later. Frances sits on the public dock picking at the splintering wood until a slice finds its way under her fingernail, waking her up from her torpor. The bay is calm; several boats cling to the municipal pier. She focuses on the gently lapping water as it kisses then withdraws from the small skiffs. Coming and going, rising and falling, a swaying metronome giving off a sweet salty smell. She hopes the salt will melt the ice of her mind so she can remember what her plan had been for today. Something to do with beautifying Sausalito.

"It's just too early to tell," she says aloud to herself, turning to see if Russell's within earshot. Russell approaches, arms full of supplies he bought at West Marine. Maybe her anchor and lead. She watches how he slowly bends, his back straight enough to ease the weight of these heavy purchases he puts into the skiff.

"That guy still on your mind?"

"Just humming a tune," she says, disregarding his question. "Got to get back to my work."

"Painting?"

"Maybe." Frances wriggles and worms. He's standing above her, peering down at her. *A woman in waiting,* she thinks, *but for what?* She wants to tell him her carefully protected heart is bleeding, but knows that's too graphic for Russell; he's a more matter-of-fact guy.

"He's upset you, hasn't he?" Russell says, lifting her chin to see a ruddy solemn face. "Is it true, what you said about killing a boy?"

She nods her head, tucking it inside her blue slicker, letting his hand stay between her chin and her neck, mumbling into it.

"Now that doesn't sound like you, Franny."

Hunched inside the blue collar, she allows his slim bent fingers to cushion her head, aware of the pulse in his hand. She breathes deeply and lays her head on his shoulder, smelling his sweet sweat. It's like a grand whisper to be held so quietly like this.

"He said she never spoke of me." When she hears her own voice, it's too loud.

"Slowly, go slowly now, Franny."

"Greg said that Anne didn't speak of me."

"That doesn't mean she doesn't think of you."

"My sister Anne is gone from me as much as the boy is."

"Are you the boy's mother?"

She nods.

"I'm sorry, Franny." Russell rocks her in his arms.

She accepts. For some time they nest on the dock, like two great sea lions. She listens to his heartbeat. The sun warms her as they move as one, gently back and forth, and when they move out of this pose, it is as easily as having moved into it. She stands up and moves toward her plan.

"Russell, you know that ugly drain pipe on Bee Street. I plan to paint it turquoise today, but not before sanding off all that rust."

"What's this, Franny? I didn't know you were a trickster!" He pinches her cheek.

"You know, I painted the public restroom near the ferry landing, don't you?"

He looks puzzled; his bushy eyebrows flare up. "I didn't know. I guess I haven't been in the women's facilities for a while," he smirks.

She laughs, feeling a little freer having confessed and been absolved.

"And today?"

"I'll be checking on the garden I planted up by the freeway. And, of course, there's the mural sketch to do."

He moves toward his vessel. "Shall I tow your dinghy in later? It seems likely you'll have a full day."

"You're so kind," she nods and waves bye, watching him motor out. Then she walks more freely toward Caledonia Street, passing the gray-yellow house where the scaffold still stands. She imagines Hernando with his family and maybe even the *jefe*. She sighs, wanting him to remember her as a feisty *abuela* like his own and not just a bag lady. She walks on past the house, past the library, up the stairway next to the drainpipe. Her painting supplies are still hidden under a rusted wheelbarrow but instead of painting the pipe now, she wants to stretch her legs, to stretch her calves and thighs up the hill. The mile-plus-some walk will do her good.

She walks past the big expensive houses that remind her of ships. Continuing on toward the electric towers, she hopes the garden she planted there two years ago is beginning to conceal them.

She remembers taking a Golden Gate Transit bus to the Mill Valley Nursery to order some flowering trees, paying cash from her Social Security account, then meeting the delivery truck a few days later in front of the tower. Twenty bucks convinced the driver to help her dig a few holes. There she planted the magnolia, camellia, and bougainvillea in hopes of obscuring the tower.

In front of them, she surveys their growth. About fifteen feet high and bushy-wide, they face her. She bows to the thriving trees, double their size, telling them of her pledge to continue these good works to beautify this town. The town fathers seem to have little interest in these projects. It's like the children's playgrounds, she thinks, not their priority.

She surveys her masterpiece, pinches a leaf from the magnolia, the leaf Nicola pointed to on the last day of his life, and puts it between her teeth. She can still see his pointer and thumb picking it up. Walking beyond the towers she moves up the remote hill toward the freeway. She relishes the wilder smell of the fresh earth—the eucalyptus and fennel enliven her senses. Fingering a piece of anise from the flowering head, she lets the aroma work its magic. The sun lowers itself, touching Mt. Tamalpais. It's getting close to five and the low sun makes it a bit chilly. She continues, crossing the path westerly. Dried leaves, grasses, and decomposing mulch cushion her feet, softening the sounds of the cars. When she reaches the summit, she feels tired from the mile walk uphill. She folds her coat as a cushion and rests with her back supported by the tree. Rocking herself the way Russell just rocked her at the dock, she falls asleep.

She wakes up to a baby's cry, insistent and urgent, tears seeming to soak through her clothes. Confused by the wetness, she forgets she's sitting in a eucalyptus grove near the freeway. It's raining. It's dark, maybe the middle of the night. But where is the baby? She opens and closes her eyes to make sure she's awake. Her body aches with fever. With each breath she shivers. Her throat feels all raw, sensitive to swallowing. She can't make out the whereabouts of the crying child as fog tumbles over the ridge and down the hill into her lap. She's sure he's there.

It's a toddler's cry. She snatches up her coat, managing to pull herself into it without falling. Slowly she makes her way down the hill, slipping in the sludge of the newly aroused earth, awakening after the long dry season. She knows she can't row out to her boat tonight in this dark and rain, so she heads to Napa Street where Malik keeps his car unlocked and parked in a seventy-two-hour zone. So generous, Malik has told her to use this space when the winds and rains keep her in town.

A quiet pervades Bridgeway; the shops are closed and the tourist traffic is gone. The dense billowing fog has drowned out the child's cry. She approaches Malik's fancy car gingerly. As always, the back door's unlocked. She slips inside the fifty-nine Olds, smelling the old leather seats, thinking she would have been fourteen when it was new, when her father would have clamored about its vanity. She covers herself with the batted comforter that lies across the back seat, putting her head down finally. With one hand in her long hair and the other resting on her heart, she falls asleep on the luxurious seat.

Is that the child banging now? She tosses and turns. The child is banging against something hard, tapping at the window. She opens her eyes to see a patrol officer shining a flashlight in her eyes.

"Ma'am, may I see your registration and license please?"

"Please go away, Officer."

"Please get out and stand by the side of the car."

"This is not my car, Officer," she says, wishing it were Margaret Bentley. Police Officer Bentley would let this pass; let her sleep out the night, only check to see she was okay. Maybe even tell her to lock the doors. Margaret Bentley watched out for Frances, waved to Frances when she walked her beat, even smiled at her. Once in a while she sat with her on the park bench as she inquired about Frances' welfare. She would have let her finish out the night there; she'd have said she was just making sure she was safe. She's always so kind. *Who is this rookie cop anyway, treating an old lady like this?*

"Please get out and place your hands on the hood of the car," he says too loud for the muffled night.

"Officer, I can explain, you don't understand that this is not my car," she says, rolling down the old window.

"All the more reason for you to come with me to the police station."

"What am I charged with? I didn't break into this car. Malik, the owner, keeps the door open and—"

"You can explain that down at the police station." He opens the car door and ushers her into the back seat of the police sedan with a slight touch on her shoulder. He puts on the spinning blue and red light as if to announce the coming of a parade and drives down Bridgeway toward Napa Street. At least he doesn't put on his siren.

She tries again to explain the agreement she has with her friend, but sees the bullet proof glass between her and the man. If only she can say it right, he'll desist, she thinks. She shouts, "I am not a vagrant. I own a boat and there is a storm tonight. Can't you see? Why don't you use your good talents and fix the parks so kids can be safe? No one gives a shit about that. Instead you mess with old ladies trying to sleep."

He takes a left-hand turn onto the dirt road where the police station is temporarily housed.

The road is bumpy and she feels aches in her body with each jounce. He parks in front of the strung-together trailers. Frances recalls the public outrage against the proposed expenditure for the new building in town that would span a public street, taking a major shortcut away from the people. The people resented the cost and rebelled, so here they were in trailers until it got sorted out.

Poor police in limbo, she thinks. *Maybe that'll knock some sense into them about what really matters.*

The officer parks in front of the main entrance and comes around to let her out. Inside the trailer is a small waiting room with a brown leather sofa and a couple of chairs, faux wood paneling on the walls. Behind a glass window sits the officer in charge, at a desk with straight-backed chairs.

Frances squints against the bright fluorescent overhead lighting. The night officer asks her to sit down, looking back toward the arresting officer who stands nearby, asking him with his eyes.

"Found her asleep in a '59 Olds. Not hers."

After they go through some rigmarole, she is free to leave the station. Officer Bentley has defended her story and Frances gets out pretty easily with a warning for vagrancy.

It's still dark outside, about 6:00 A.M., though it looks like midnight. More than a month beyond the autumn equinox, the November days bring more darkness than light. The sky has cleared and she sees the marvelous Big Dipper standing on the low side of its cup. She wants to jump up and reach for it and hop from one star to the next, tracing the lower cube and then up onto the handle, but where would she go from there? It would be like jumping without a parachute.

On the bay, diving birds soar. She envies them, grateful for their distraction. A solo sailboat motors in the channel, heading toward the Golden Gate, brightening her mood. She remembers Russell, who offered yesterday to bring in her dinghy. Was it only yesterday?

Her muscles ache, gripped by flu. Exhausted and hungry, she heads for the only café open this early, steaming chai available every morning. She slips inside like a mouse, not disturbing Sali, who works in the kitchen. Frances helps herself to a chai from a prepared thermos. Six thirty, still dark. She sits in the corner, inhaling the steam from her hot drink while she lets the cup warm her hands.

Otto enters the place with his pushcart. He doesn't see her in the corner and settles himself at the table nearest the tea counter. She watches him fill his cup with tea and add sugar. The stream of sugar spills into his cup. She's surprised, but then Otto loves salted caramel chocolate candies. When he turns, he sees her and walks slowly across the small room to where she sits.

"May I?" He places his swollen hand on her shoulder. "You don't look well."

"A bug of some sort."

"I see it in your eyes. They're peaked and red." He slides his hand to her forehead. "You have a fever."

"Warm, but I feel cold. It came to me out of the blue."

"Like your brother."

"My brother?"

"I wasn't sure you found him. You never said," Otto pulls on his white beard.

"Well, he's a brother of sorts, I never tell—"

"We never talk of families. I never told you that I have a lost brother, lost in the war. But that's for another day. Did he find you?"

"He found me. Both times on the public pier." Otto raises his bushy white eyebrows. "He's my sister's husband. She's seven years younger than me, and he is ten."

Otto laughs, "Then she was a change-of-life baby."

"Maybe so. My mother was surprised and I was surprised my mother was still having sex."

"People are funny," Otto says.

"Well, we are a Catholic family. Sex is a big secret. And I don't think my mother liked sex all that much. She didn't say; it was just the way they argued all the time. Not much affection between them either."

"And that guy, he acted like he owned you."

"Well, he doesn't but once . . . we had sex once." How quickly this comes out, after being held in for years, surprises her. She looks to see if others are listening.

"And sex with your sister's husband is a bigger secret."

"More than you know."

"Adultery, isn't it?" Otto says.

It feels like a slap. Frances looks away, buries herself in her chai. "Incest, the greatest taboo for a Catholic family, for all families, isn't it?"

"Other than killing a man."

She's so deep in her memories, her guilt, that she doesn't hear him. She envisions the words in the Catholic catechism, the sixth commandment of God: "Thou shalt not commit adultery." It's infinitely worse, too, that he was her brother-in-law. This is an offense against a sacred contract of marriage. She feels the gravity of her behavior and shivers against the cold feeling piercing through her heated body. Would some call it incest? She hopes not, as she remembers the fine print about incest in the Catholic catechism, about how "incest corrupts and regresses one to animality."

When she looks up, Otto is staring at her. They look at each other until the sound of the door opening breaks their lock. She spots Russell, wearing his rubber boots, heading for the coffee. He's dressed the part of a sailor who has just experienced the first rain. He warms himself over the pots like they are the fire his body needs. When he turns, he sees them huddled at the corner seat and walks over.

"You look like you've seen a ghost," Russell says to Frances.

Frances turns away from Otto and toward Russell, who does not say any more but takes her hands and begins to rub them to get them warm.

10

General Delivery

After breakfast Frances hangs out in the children's play-ground, watching mothers and babies at the park below the library where the infant seats are intact. Precious babies swing toward their moms and then swing away. Come and go, come and go. They are smiling, reaching, even laughing. She sits on the bench feeling the cold on her butt. Her child came and went and she feels as cold as the bench that holds her. If only she could have seen more clearly. It was to be no come and go for her child, only go. Why?

She spends the day in the library in a state halfway between reading the *Chronicle* and falling asleep. When she finally moves to leave, the light has shifted and the library crowd is now the after-work crowd. She decides to check her mailbox before going to La Stella where her friends hang out.

Her mailbox contains a letter addressed in her name, sent General Delivery. She carefully holds the onion-skinned paper envelope and reads:

Frances Pia
General Delivery
Sausalito, CA
November

She rubs her finger over the smooth silky paper, the saffron postage stamp, feeling, waiting, wanting and not wanting to open it, wondering if Anne licked the envelope the way she used to as a child. But Anne is in India, so far away. Frances seems incapable of believing a letter would arrive four weeks later. Frances carefully opens the flap and reads.

Varanasi India
Dear Frances,

It's night in Varanasi where I sit on the steps of the Ganges River. Dark except for the rings of fire around the six monks who pray and give thanks for the end of another day. As for me, all is black, except for the cremation fires on the hillside, constantly reminding me of my own loss. All I can think of in this dark river place is that I never could conceive a child with Greg. You had the child I never could. You have a growing son. I have nothing. I can't bear it, Franny. I never had a baby. And now I'm too old.

Frances looks up. It's unfathomable that Anne doesn't know of Nicola's death, as if that knowledge would soothe Anne's emptiness. How crazy this thought seems. She feels muddled that what burns and chars her might somehow make Anne feel comforted. She reads on.

> *You're the one who was always the good one, the oldest, the nun, the scholar, the artist, and then the mother. You always got what you wanted, Franny. You're watching your boy grow and I have nothing.*

Frances fumbles with the letter, folding it almost to a crumple and stuffs it into her pocket. *How can it be possible that Greg didn't tell her? Again I trusted him. How could I?* Panic of losing Anne grips Frances. Her hands shake and her heart pulls tight, seeming to shorten her breath. Her boy is dead. It never ceases to amaze her, when the God-given panic sets in, how dangerous it all feels. All she wants to do is run, but where? To her boat? To loneliness? After all the years the panic is still there. She cannot hide from it.

How has this happened, dear Lord? How could I ever think for a moment she would forgive me? I hoped she might. After all is done I am a cheat, a whore, and guilty of lust. What about my vows of poverty, chastity and obedience?

Worry whirls within her, churning her insides. She pulls her coat under her to feel its warmth. Frances finds herself sitting on the stoop outside the post office, her hand squeezing the onion-skinned paper in her pocket. She sees Anne at the river's edge, reliving some ancient ritual. She wishes she were there sitting beside her on the Ganges and not in this godforsaken cold.

Anne doesn't know we are both childless. Frances' mind is like a loop. Her boy is dead and Anne is childless too. A strange heaviness swells her insides. "We are both childless," she says aloud, allowing it to sink in.

The grief, like ocean waves breaking out of a dam, crushes her spirits. *Poor Anne,* Frances thinks. *I have caused this suffering.*

How has this happened, dear Lord? How could I ever think for a moment she would forgive me? She waits, as if He'll answer. *How could she have come here to see me, thinking I was living all this time in Sausalito with my son?* She slips into her coat to feel its warmth at her neck and reads the last lines of Anne's letter.

> *No-see-ums hovered above me, threatening to bite, and the Doms tended the dead. And the sweet man gave me tea. Franny, your candle spilled over but I don't want you to die. You looked so old and disheveled.*

Frances doesn't know how long she sits there. Time telescopes the past and then zooms in on the present moment so that it's all the same. It's late when she continues on her walk, crossing Bridgeway toward her evening meal at La Stella's. Her heart feels heavy, and she wants to get to her boat to sleep, but she knows she must eat first.

11

Blackie's Pasture

It's well after 8:00 P.M. when she enters the crowded restaurant and looks around for her friends. Russell's not there; Otto's elsewhere. She hopes Malik will be in the back room, sitting at his usual table away from the piano. Walking toward his table, she sees him twirling linguine on his fork. She sits at a table kitty-corner from him.

"Heavy gusts tonight, Fran. Beginning at 10:00 P.M. You're welcome to spend the night in the Olds."

"Do I dare, after last night?"

"I told them you have my permission."

"Maybe I should get it in writing and have it notarized."

"Protecting the public. That's all, Fran."

"You think?"

Umberto interrupts. "Chicken *rosemarino* tonight, *Signora.*"

She nods. "And a glass of Chianti, please." He pours the red wine into the glass. A sip soothes her throat and washes away the dread of the day and the fear of another night like the last.

Malik finishes his pasta and pushes away his dish, leaving a twenty. "Enjoy and watch out, Fran."

The waiter places the steaming chicken dish before her. Scents of rosemary remind her of Anne. Though her mouth waters, she postpones her indulgence by sitting silently another moment, putting off her urge to devour the food. Remembering Anne's letter, she feels undeserving of this meal. She finishes the wine. When she finally tastes the rosemary and garlic, she eats ravenously, assimilating the familial flavors.

"Eh!" Umberto says, hanging around her first bite, bringing his thumb and fingers together near his right cheek and shaking them back and forth, as if to say, *what do you expect?*

"Another chianti, *per favore.*"

"Coming up for the *principessa,*" Umberto teases, pouring the dark ruby wine into the gigantic goblet. "Drink, *Signora.*"

"I love life tonight," she squeals, draining the second glass. Then she experiences a lightness in her neck, shoulders, and back. A warmth, heretofore absent.

"*Beata lei.* Lucky you. *La Signora* loves life," Umberto says, raising his glass. For a moment Frances feels blessed by the waiter, by the wine, until she remembers the small craft warnings told by Malik. It's a quarter to ten. She quickly pays and leaves the restaurant. Autumn leaves swirl on the sidewalk, but not more than usual.

She makes a deal with herself. *If the water's calm, I'll head out; if not, I'll wait for Russell and hitch a ride.* When she gets to the pier, she surmises the situation. The water on this side of the bay is calm, but then the channel itself could surprise her. Russell's boat is still tied up, so he's in town and she could wait for him. Otto's already anchor out. Malik's warning. *Bah! Just do it. No whitecaps here.* The masts on the larger craft rock gently, sending their bell sounds to lull her like the church bells. She gets her dinghy.

Peering across the channel, she barely makes out her anchorage, but then she usually can't see it from the shore. She looks at her watch; it isn't ten as yet. If she could just make it to her boat, she could withstand the night and the winds that would make the sailboat rock and roll, better than Malik's car again or the police station. *Those cops are cracking down on anchor outs.*

Knowing Russell has laid her new anchor gives her a sense of safety. She unties the skiff from the cleat, takes hold of her oars, and gently pushes off the dock, angling a slight diagonal. In the channel she notices the outgoing tide pulling her toward her boat. She can even see her red balloon buoy bobbing as she crosses. She pictures herself attaching to the stern and pulling herself up the ladder and into her boat.

She pulls hard, adjusts her angle, and proceeds diagonally, passing Marker Four. Just as she nears her boat, a gust of wind swerves her away, sending cold splashes of water into her face, making her squint. She misses the mark, overshoots, and bypasses her anchorage. The clanking of nearby masts floods her ears now. She looks at the defunct engine on the back of the dinghy, useless, yet she still believes she'll make it. But the west wind and the ebb pull her toward Raccoon Strait, away from her vessel.

Given the short distance from her craft to the strait, she begins her row, knowing she must avoid the dangerous rocks at Belvedere Point and at the same time make the turn into the strait. The ebb will want to take her to the other side, toward the Gate.

The wind whips at her face while waves, perpendicular to her bow, slam into her, crashing over the bow, bringing water into the dinghy. "Sailor, beware," she says out loud. She feels alert and strong; maybe it's the blast of cold water. She readies herself for the possible and impossible demands that await her. Gripping the oars tightly, she recalls Russell bending into his skiff with her new anchor and lines, his body mechanics so graceful and long, and how he prepared her sailboat for just this day. But he's not here to keep her safe. She's alone in a small dinghy with a defunct motor—useless to have it bobbing and wagging, throwing things off-balance.

She looks at her oarlocks and hopes they are sturdy enough, that she won't flip one overboard. But they are now extensions of her hands and arms and torso and waist and legs and calves and ankles and cold toes. Every movement is animalistic, pushing her to survive.

She rows, seeing the dark mass of the point approaching quickly in front of her. She rows, pulling a hard right, hoping to make a loop around the rocks and into the straight, but the wind pushes her toward the bay and into the ebb. A whirlpool of water jerks her around, splashing over the sides of her small boat. The cold water drips over her face, stinging her eyes and filling her mouth with salt.

What if I let go of the oars right here and let it take me at its will? Let it covet me. Let it consume me as I consume it into my being.

The oneness with the sea, the Great Mother, grips her as strongly as she grips the oars. Straining, she pulls the water hard to starboard around the mass and left into the tunnel of the fast-moving strait. She has the feeling that she is in the center of a massive curling wave, the center of a storm with an unfathomable calmness, a blue peace like the Virgin Mary, a tunnel which will keep her safe and dry. "Are you calling me, Dear Mother Mary, to become one with the eternal sea?" She asks, "Am I dead?"

Not yet.

A wave slaps over the bow as she moves close to the rocks and into the strait, bringing in more water over her toes. She searches her mind for a bucket to bail her boat, but this is not the time. She must hold onto the oars. She digs her heels in and points her toes up and rows. The cold water laps her sandaled toes. She knows she must get round the bend without crashing into the rocks, so she adjusts her direction, making a wider turn at Belvedere Point, and then heads as close as she can to the black landmass without getting swept into the rocks. She pulls hard, but it's as if she is standing still, doing calisthenics on a stationary machine. But she is rowing with all her strength. *You'll make it. Keep rowing, Frances, don't stop until you make the current.* Her strength wavers, but the coach inside helps her to keep it up. *You can do it. You can do it.* She keeps up the rigorous rowing, her heart drumming.

The boat is moving forward now, close to the shore, a safe enough distance between the monolithic rocks and the tidal ebb.

She had been careless tonight, ignoring the warnings, and now she would be tested. *I am in Your hands, dear Lord; I surrender to Your will for me. How could I ever doubt You?* She feels her strength resurge and she rows and rows and rows. Her upper arms engage with her hands and the paddles. Her whole body works with the sea itself to move her smoothly toward the safe harbor. Close to the shoreline and safely away from the competing currents and rocks, she rows toward the small harbor at Sam's Restaurant. All she has to do is to keep up her energy and stay close to shore.

She sees Russell in her mind and smiles to herself at the way he pinches her cheeks and calls her Franny, the way he cups her body, and the way he fitted her sailboat for the storm. She licks her salty lips, tasting his, as she ties up at Sam's.

It's 11:00. An hour has passed—an hour that seems like eternity. When she gets to the restaurant, late stragglers hang out at the bar, laughing and drinking; waiters and busboys do their last chores. Frances slips into the restroom and places herself in front of the hand drier to get warm. She stares at her image in the mirror. She sees a ruddy-faced, red-nosed sixty-year-old woman with a wild thick head of red and white hair. Medusa. She stares at this wild woman. *Who are you?* She looks deeply into her own eyes. Deep vast blue, as deep as the sea. *Who am I?*

After waiting at a bus stop for a few minutes, she realizes the bus service has stopped. It's late. She walks inland away from the main street so that she can be near the inlets of the bay, where to her surprise the water is still, black like slate. Deeply beautiful. *Hard to believe it's the same sea.* She passes the two yacht clubs, staying on a street that parallels the main boulevard into Tiburon. It's quiet as she surveys the picturesque houses so near to the water. It'll take a good hour to reach Blackie's Pasture, a park now two miles away. Tired, she pushes herself forward one foot at a time past Blackie's Pasture, remembering the dear horse she used to pat as a child, a swayback named Blackie.

As she nears the Pasture on the corner of Tiburon Boulevard, a police car with flashing lights pulls up beside her.

"May I see your identification, please?"

"I don't have any, Officer."

"What are you doing out here by yourself, walking at midnight?"

"I'm walking to Sausalito where I live."

"How'd you get out here by the freeway?"

"The gale took me off my mark. My dinghy is tied up at Sam's, Officer."

"You've been drinking. I can smell the wine on your breath."

"Wine with dinner."

He raises his eyebrows. "No one in their right mind would paddle across Raccoon Strait in this storm. Please get in." He ushers her toward the rear door. She hates his hand on her elbow and, even more, that he doesn't believe her. She pushes away from him. In the mix they scuffle. She feels trapped and confined. Her heart races. His hands stick to her arms. As she tries to pry herself away by an upward arm gesture coming from her center, she scratches him, which results in him tackling her and pulling her toward the car.

"It's for your own good, Ma'am," he says pushing her into the back seat of the black and white. "We're going to the police station for the night, Ma'am."

"You can't do that. Take your hands off me!" she demands. "And what for?"

"For tackling an officer, for starters."

"That's not my intention. I just want to get back home and you won't let me. My good friend Officer Margaret Bentley will explain to you, sir. She knows me and she's the Sausalito Police Chief."

"You have a right to talk about that at the county jail."

He steps away from the car to talk into his walkie talkie. He's walking toward the other side of the car.

She runs toward the railroad trestle, knowing all the nooks and crannies, trees and bushes in the field from childhood hide and seek games.

Passing in the shadow of the statue of Blackie, a memorial to a horse that lived in the field when she was a child. She hides in the estuary under the bridge with her feet in the water. The foghorns spilling out their melancholy *Brooooooooooooom-druuuuuuuuuuuuuuuum*, sounds like the chant of the temple bell to her ears. She prays for the thick and alive moisture to save her from the cop. The virtues of the fog fill her heart and cool her skin. She closes her eyes, imagining the old horse, Blackie, remembering how he swam from Tiburon across the bay to San Francisco's Crissy Field in twenty-three minutes, winning a bet placed on him by his owner. Briefly she considers swimming as a possibility for her, then dismisses it. The water is black, cold, and harsh. Her feet and calves are numb. She wriggles her feet and ankles, keeping her blood circulating, bracing herself against the cold as fear grips her insides.

She thinks of Anne in the Ganges where they do cremations. The heat of the image warms her heart. There the Doms tend the dead. Do they tend the living? And the police, do they tend the living? She doesn't want to die tonight, hiding under a bridge like a troll. Blackie's field seems much too small for Frances' adult body. She worries the incoming tide will rise and drown her. Shivering, stretching her legs, hopping from one foot to another, memories of her dead mother and father grip her heart. In the cold damp darkness, she touches the slimy seaweed ropes that cling to the underside of the bridge, like the tangles inside her. Then wonders if this is hell on earth, her own River Styx. The familiar self-talk inside her head begins.

You, dear Lord, are asking me to grow muscles? Again. And again. Is this what You meant for me? I can't do this any-more. I'm a coward who can't face my demons. I want to run away. Aren't I a con artist, a fugitive woman? I left Anne when she needed me. I killed the baby.

No, you are a Catholic nun and have a penchant for lying to yourself! You should be ashamed of yourself. A yellow-bellied coward, living in a shroud, not even a veil. The Doms tend the dead. The police want me out of the way. No-see-ums hovered above me and the sweet man gave me tea. Franny, your candle spilled over but I don't want you to die. You looked so old and disheveled.

These words jumble around—*Your candle spilled over*—as the waves swish at her knees and thighs in the cold waters. *She wants me dead. Anne wants me dead, or why would she tell me my candle spilled over? Oh, miserable me, how can I go on living knowing Anne wants me dead?* Frances goes over and over this thought and carries it to her next place.

One o'clock, early morning. She leaves Blackie's pasture, walking close to the water, believing the cops have given up on her. With luck it'll take her forty-five minutes to get to Strawberry Village and then an hour and fifteen from there to get to Sausalito. Two more hours in the cold night. She'll make it a vigil. She thinks of Our Lady or Lourdes and all the pil-grims. *I am a pilgrim, Dear Mother Mary, please keep me safe.*

She hugs the shoreline, passing condos and houses, the Marin Audubon, and eventually cuts through a schoolyard, then another residential area and a ballpark before she gets to the shopping center at Strawberry. Reaching Strawberry, she

takes her rosary from her pocket, blesses herself in the name
of the Father and prays on the pearl rosary, fingering each
bead, repeating a Hail Mary on each pearl, going through
each decade in prayerful meditation, including the sorrowful
and joyful mysteries. Over and over, *Hail Mary, full of grace.*
The Lord is with thee. Pray for my sins, now and at the hour
of my death. One step at a time and one bead at a time, she
makes the five-mile pilgrimage. She's nearly home now, back
to Sausalito and the storage shed on the dock. Her boat will
have to be retrieved tomorrow.

At 3:00 A.M. Frances opens the door to her locker on
the pier, something she's done every day for three years.
The metal latch and chain feel rough tonight, and cold to
the touch. They are loosely attached to the metal knob as
if someone has pried them. She jangles the chain, pulling it
easily out from its source. The ease, the looseness, alert her
as it slides away from the door, making her wonder if she
forgot to securely fasten the lock. *What if someone is hiding*
inside? With the chain in her hand she opens the door, reaching inside the shed, feeling past an oar for the light switch.
But she stops herself from turning on the switch, not wanting
to alert any possible cops on night watch.

The wind on the bay picks up, sending a blast of cold
damp air through her tweed skirt and woolen sweater, prick-
ling her bare legs. How could she be so stupid to have missed
her mark and been taken out toward Raccoon Strait?

She goes over the sequence of events that evening, making her stomach turn. The light switch behind the oar seems
to vibrate as she touches it, sending a twitch of electric shock
to her cold hands. The jarring vibration keeps pace with the
wind whistling through the cracks of the cubicle. She pushes

into the shed, hoping there will be enough room for her to stretch out her body. She wants to sleep, to get out of the cold, to get away from the peering eyes of the police who have been watching her, threatening to send her to a shelter.

She hears footsteps on the dock as she quickly squeezes into the darkened shed. The oar sticks into her back as she flattens herself against the narrow wall of the cubicle and holds her breath. How had it come to this? How had she fallen from grace—an educated woman stealing away in a tiny footlocker? She holds her breath.

"Open up, Frances," comes the deep voice from outside. She holds her stomach in, feeling it close to her back, not daring to exhale. She listens. She can almost hear him breathing.

"She's in there, Mac. I saw her enter somewhere around here," says a younger voice. "Let's break the door in. She's been evading us."

Frances listens as they talk about her. What did they know about her anyway? They couldn't see she was doing her best, that she had a series of bad luck experiences. And what did they know, such young pricks? How could they even contemplate that she didn't deserve her freedom?

With the oar stiff at her back, she breathes gently, listening for the men's voices. They are gone or hushed now in the foggy night. She hears the first horn off the gate. The first blast bellows a deep and haunting sound—*brooooooooooo droooooooooooooooooom*. She counts, *One, two.* Then the pause. Could it be ten seconds long? She waits to hear the second blast of a higher pitched horn. Then another. A kind of symphony on the bridge with each horn speaking to the next, melting into the responding other. Once again their timbre soothes her as it must soothe other navigators.

She slides herself down the oar, feeling each vertebrae vibrating against the giant wooden arm until her lower back rests on the widest part. She lets the hand of the paddle cup her sacrum. With her bent knees next to her breasts and her feet flat on the plywood floor of the footlocker, she rests her head on her knees and falls asleep, drop-dead tired, in a few seconds.

•   •   •

Sometime in the early morning, she wakes to the squeal of a mouse who seems as surprised as she to find her there. The blessed foghorns orient her. She hears the two horns that blow simultaneously—a two-second blast is then followed by eighteen seconds off. Then the repeat. She knows they live on the South Tower of the Golden Gate Bridge. She remembers she isn't in her boat but on the pier. She shivers as she recalls her seven-mile journey to Tiburon and back. Had she really walked all that way?

"I'm hiding in a footlocker," she says to no one, slowly opening the door onto the dock, walking into the night and into the hands of the two officers who apparently decided to wait it out for her. *Bless their souls,* she thinks, *they've been up all night, too, doing their work. They don't give up, do they?* They walk toward her.

She makes an immediate about face and starts to run, but her muscles are wobbly and betray her. They reach her and have her in a hold. She doesn't have much to give as push back, except to use her tongue as a weapon.

"Keep your hands off me, you snakes," she spits.

Each of the policemen holds an arm. "You're sleeping the

rest of the night off in the station," says the one she scratched earlier. He smirks at her like she's some piece of crap.

"Can't you leave an old sailor alone? What the fuck!" She squirms. "Don't you have anything better to do with your night? Get your hands off me. I'm making a citizen's arrest at your abuse of an old lady."

"Now calm down, Ma'am, no need for that kind of talk," the second one says.

She has the urge to scratch him too, so he matches the other one. Two twisted men of the law don't really seem to know how to help.

Feeling sorry for herself, she wishes the sea had taken her last night, imagining the blue light to be the Great Mother wave curling itself around her with its calm tunnel-like center. She sees herself floating on a long narrow canal alone in a serene silence, gliding toward a doorway into another world, another world where Nicola waits for her.

They take her to the police car and then the station house. She's so tired she lets them.

•   •   •

Frances opens her eyes against the light, realizing she's lying on a cot in a strange room. She squints her lids open and shut, kicking the woolen blanket that loosely covers her. *Where the hell am I?* Rolling onto her side with her arms wrapped around her head, rough fingers covering her eyes, she makes a cocoon, allowing the image of soft blue light to protect her. She wants to hold onto that image, but it's slipping away out of reach. She rolls the opposite way as if she might find it there. When the bed cover slips to the floor she shivers, grabs for it, and pulls it up over her eyes, a respite that lasts only until she realizes her feet are sticking out of the bottom of the bed. "Damn! Will I ever get any peace?"

She bends her knees so all her body is hidden under the blanket. For a moment she finds stillness until she kicks out and the blanket falls to the floor. She looks over the edge of the bed at a cream-colored, plasticized wooden floor she doesn't recognize. She pinches up her nose and looks from side to side, stopping at the foot of the bed where two sandals, one flipped on its side, rest. Had she walked last night in sandals like the dear Christ at Calvary? The horrific night of danger floods her mind. Why hadn't He taken her then? What is her destiny? For a brief minute she contemplates having given in, letting go the oars, letting herself be consumed by the water. She envisions a bloated body floating out to sea or worse, hung up on the Belvedere Point, being smashed by the currents but still in the shadow.

Imagining herself on the rocks, she contemplates her soul. Where would it be? Not with the bloated body. She thinks of Nicola. If she leaves, who will remember him? The thought of nothingness is scarier than the thought of killing herself.

The mortal sin of suicide will cost too much. The salvation of her soul and maybe Nic's. Then the calming words of the Catholic Catechism come to her. *We shall not despair of eternal salvation of persons who have taken their own lives for they don't know, they're not in their right mind.*

Yet, at the same time, living feels intolerable. *The Doms tend the dead*, Anne's words run through her mind. Then she remembers her mother saying, "They shoot horses don't they?" Oh, her thoughts run all together like gobbledygook, tangling and sticking to her mind. Her words bounce off the walls of the tiny room. Is she talking to herself or to God?

Better for the good Lord to change His mind and take her soon.

"Why must I live? Please let go of me, let me sleep, dear Lord. I am a poor soldier of this life."

She sits up, pressing her hands on her woolen tweed skirt, running them up and down, placing her hand under her floppy hairy sweater, moving slowly on upward, stopping at her breast, remembering Nic's ashes. Her hand opens and closes, squeezing the blue silk pouch holding his ashes warmed by her breasts. She speaks aloud to his ashes.

"Nicola, while I'm still here on this earth, I'll keep you alive, not to worry," she says, imagining him smiling. Looking toward the ray of light shining on her feet, she follows it on upward to a high, barred window.

Her mouth opens wide; her eyebrows lift in some recognition after the thought of Nic. A fury kicks the covers. *How in Hell's name did I get here? I'm not meant to be barred and caged. Who the hell's plan is this? Here I am, a woman religious, who just fought the waves and currents in Richardson Bay, and what for? To be jailed in a cell with barred windows and a plastic floor?*

•   •   •

Frances puckers her lips as she stares at the six black pieces of metal that bar the small rectangular window. She's bouncing like a kid, her left hand on the mattress, and her butt in the air. When her feet fall off the side of the bed to the floor, she jumps again, dancing a jig on the cold floor as her hands wave side to side. She blows on each of them and dances around the bed, looking down and under for something.

Then she gets down on her knees and searches under the

bed and pulls at something, pulling, pulling, pulling a long red woolen coat. She brings it up to her nose. It's her familiar smell like her boat. The Nivea cream she wears on her old chapped hands mixes with the wood smell of the boat and the fumes from her Evinrude to create the smell of Frances. She sits up and hugs the coat to her lap, then brings it close to her face, smelling and nuzzling it in an inordinate way before putting it on. Her eyes softly close and her mouth relaxes as she fingers the smooth beads in her pocket. Stillness. "Thank you," she mutters.

After a few moments she picks herself up from the cot, puts on her coat and her shoes, and faces the sun. "Eastern mountain bites the sun," a Zen saying she's learned in her studies. Face the day! Her words seem to echo off the walls. For a moment she thinks someone is talking back to her, mimicking. She looks around to see if there might be someone listening to her ramblings. Safe, she's alone.

She grabs the foot of the bed with both hands, holding onto each leg, and pulls the bed against the wall beneath the window, screeching the metal against the shiny plastic-wood floor. Her lips make a tight line across her face, screeching silently with the bed. Then she steps up onto the foot of the bed and reaches toward the bars. Her foot slips off the sheet and she falls to the floor. *Is this how Christ felt when He carried the cross the last mile?* Her head bows as she sits there huddled in her red blanket coat, rubbing her hip, thinking of Christ's agony in the garden, for which He too must have felt betrayed. *Had He ever thought of suicide?*

More determined to succeed, she pulls herself up onto the mattress, kneeling into its center. She bows her head and rounds her shoulders and waits bent like this before looking up toward the bars. One foot at a time, she carefully stands up and reaches toward the window, holding onto the bars, hoisting herself up so her sandaled feet are midair. Her eyes are above the sill, her head and red body suspended by her arms. She hangs there silently, on her own cross, waiting.

Frances is still suspended when the door to the cell room opens. She doesn't move as she stares at a eucalyptus tree gently waving above her head. She hears footsteps in the room.

"Hey, Frances. It's Margaret Bentley. May I sit down?" She takes a seat on the bed.

Frances doesn't answer, feeling humiliated by her own image—a woman hanging from the bars with her feet dangling above the bed; one sandal slipped off. She sways her legs and watches one hundred band-tailed pigeons take flight. A raven soars in front of them, heading for the tallest perch, screeching as he goes. As Frances lets go and falls down, the bird caws and the bed squeals, a cacophony. She feels the muscle strain in her arms from hanging so long as she lands on the bed next to Margaret and stares.

"You've had a rough night. I hear you were out in the storm." Frances bites her lower lip.

Margaret gently rests her hand on Frances' shoulder as they sit together in silence. Frances' nose is running, and she looks for a tissue. She smoothes out her coat under her and bends to retrieve her overturned sandal.

"You'll be okay," Margaret hands Frances a tissue.

Frances looks toward Margaret, wiping her nose. "Is it okay to be a woman living alone? Why must people be blamed for their lifestyle?"

"Tell me, Frances, who is blaming you?"

"Those damn cops are blaming me, for one," she snaps.

"And who else?"

"God is blaming me."

"Are you hearing voices?" Margaret asks.

Frances doesn't know for sure. She looks at Margaret and takes a deep slow breath. "Like the cycles of the tides, highs and lows flow through me, Margaret. The suffering of human-kind—I feel it." She doesn't want to think she's been talking to the walls, that she's had enough, that life exhausts her, that she's a coward and doesn't have the courage that life demands. Frances hopes Margaret doesn't ask her to explain her dark thoughts, or tell her once again how she suffers from a mental illness. What did they call it? Bipolar? So cold, the word makes her shiver. She pulls her red blanket coat tightly around her torso.

"You're having a rough patch right now, that's all."

Frances keeps quiet, hoping not to divulge her innermost thoughts about wanting to swallow the ocean or be swallowed by it. *This is not confession but survival,* she tells herself.

The policewoman adjusts the buckle of her belt, shifting her weight on the low mattress.

"All my life I've struggled. It first started when I was away from home in Italy. I had bouts of crying. I thought it was homesickness. Hmm!" She hums, pursing her lips together.

"It's likely; you were so far from your family," Margaret says. "I don't think I could manage that." Margaret listens, her hands open and relaxed in her lap.

"Always the trials. Last night the real highs and lows of the tides nearly ran me adrift on the rocks at the point. But by the grace of God I made it to Tiburon. You see, Margaret, it's God's way—always the trials. I've learned to sail with them."

"You sure are sailing with them. Officer Clement told me how you missed your anchor and ended up heading toward Tiburon in the dark of night with the winds gusting. Is it true?"

"The truth. The dark night of the soul."

Margaret looks puzzled. "I don't know what that means."

"Prevailing winds, that's all." Frances wonders if she's said something crazy. But she dismisses it, knowing that nonreligious people might not know about St. John of the Cross and his poem, *The Dark Night of the Soul*, worse than Dante's *Inferno*.

"Now I'm here, Margaret. Seems unfair to be treated like a criminal when all I was doing was walking home."

"That's true, you weren't harming anyone." She looks into Frances' eyes.

Frances pulls back, fearing Margaret can see into her wounded soul. Would she see Medusa, one of the three monstrous sisters with snakes coming out of her head and tusks for teeth, the face she remembers seeing last night in the mirror at Sam's? An evil deformed sister who could turn whoever gazed at her into stone. She holds her hands over her eyes as much to hide herself as to protect Margaret. For a moment she believes she has this power. Frances doesn't want to see her own face, a face of guilt and exaggerated sorrow.

She tries to normalize her thoughts. But she can't stop seeing the doctor at psych emergency—the one she saw three months ago—who was talking to her about mood disorders. She can still see him tapping the cover of the diagnostic manual as if he needed some validation for prescribing his drugs.

"Ugh!" she says.

What would he say now? He'd be suggesting a hypomanic episode. She remembered the words—*a distinct period of abnormally and persistently elevated, expansive, or irritable mood lasting at least one week*. He talked like that, straight out of his diagnostic manual. Was it that simple?

She feels offended at the suggestion her life might be whittled down to a diagnostic category. In her mind's eye the section titles glare at her. Mania and depression ring loud in her ears; she covers them with both hands. She doesn't want Margaret to hear.

"No," she counters, "the dark night of the soul, that's all, the dark night of the soul."

"I'd like to hear what you are saying, you're mumbling." Margaret says.

"It's just a Catholic thing. I read once about the journey of a soul, but where was I?" she asks, wanting to change the subject, wanting to tell her the details. "I seem to have lost my place." She holds her fingers tightly as if the answer is there. "Yes, last night. Last night began with a dinner at La Stella, drinking wine like others do. Then it all went south. Two nights in a row I'm bothered by the police."

"I'm sorry, Frances, we'll look into their behavior," Margaret says, "but I'm concerned about your safety."

Frances likes the validation and takes a deeper breath. Her fingers relax, no longer a tight fist.

"Frances, how'd you come to live anchor out instead of having a house on land?"

"It saves my life to live anchor out. Every day it saves my life." The policewoman raises her eyebrows in a question, seeming not to understand. "Maybe it's the same reason you carry that gun."

They sit silently on the low prison mattress staring at each other.

"Last night when I was close to my demons and my angels, I told myself we got to love our demons as much as our angels. Do you see?"

"I'm not sure," says Margaret. "Are you hearing voices? If so, you're going to need help."

"Retrieving my skiff?"

"More than that, Frances. I'm concerned about your judgment."

"I wasn't drunk. I had a drink with dinner, but I got myself safely to Tiburon and walked five hard miles."

"It might be time to consider living in a house on land."

"I don't want to hear that, Margaret." She fidgets, hating the feeling of being trapped. Without the sea she feels cribbed. She squirms away and looks up toward the barred window where at least the light of the day shines through.

"I'll ask Russell to help me out," she says. She bows in front of Officer Bentley, who stands up in front of her. Frances feels afraid that this woman, in her eagerness to be helpful, will chain her to convention like the others are trying to do. They all want to lock her up and throw away the key. She stands up, irritated. She must get out of here and fast.

"Frances, one more thing before I let you go. Are you taking your meds?" she asks.

"I'm okay now."

"Are you still taking your meds?" the woman asks again.

"Yeah yeah, I've been to Marin General for my refill," she lies. She hates the way the medication makes her feel numb, the way her creativity is compromised for some stability. She wants to see the color and hear the music. She hates the way Officer Bentley thinks that medication is the answer to her life.

"You're kind to me, Margaret, not like the others." Frances masks her worry about what Margaret might do to her, fearing she has seen too closely.

12

A Tangled Tango

Before Frances leaves the police station, she splashes icy cold water on her face and inhales the strong disinfectant smells in the restroom, allowing the astringent to penetrate her nostrils. She walks quickly toward Caledonia Street, hoping to find Otto or Russell in the café. Her muscles ache with a cramping tightness in her calves. If only she could massage them, but she dare not stop here in the street. At least there's a reason for this physical pain after the long row, the walk, the sleep in the storage shed and the cell. Her stomach growls in protest. She hasn't eaten, only sipped that black coffee at the station.

She scans the street, looking for shadows, expecting them everywhere. *No black and whites—safe for the moment,* she thinks. She rushes, intent on being within the safety net of her friends. Running now, she dashes into the small café on Caledonia Street, out of breath. It's quiet and dark inside. She can hear her own breathing. Sali works in the tiny kitchen with large steaming pots of tea misting up the place, reminding her of the dear fog that saved her life last night. She sits down in the far corner with a filled cup, inhaling the steam, letting the mug warm her hands.

Otto comes in but doesn't see her as he arranges his hat on the bench diagonally across from her. He takes off his woolen jacket before he sits down. She can smell the damp rich wool of his moist clothes permeating the steam in the small space and mixing with the coffee and spiced chai, making a unique masala.

The woolen knickers Otto wears are part of his winter uniform, and a carryover from his youth. They hold an underlying odor of the sheep from which they were sheared, but Otto had not been a farmer. Otto was a skier in Norway of Olympian caliber. He rarely speaks of those days, except to say he would ski on rare hot spring days down the alpine slopes facing the fjords, shirtless. She squints at him, trying to picture a buff young man; he would be sleek, tanned, and muscular, wearing those same knee-high pants. She doesn't doubt he was capable of such antics.

Frances follows his movements at the tea counter, letting his methodical ways give some order to her state. He takes the sugar jug and pours a white stream into his tea. When he turns, he sees her and walks the hypotenuse of the triangle of the small square room, taking the most direct path toward her. He stops in front of her, looks into her eyes, and places a large roughened hand on her shoulder, which presses her down just enough for her to feel settled for the first time all day. She stares into his eyes, letting them revive her from the cold night of despair and worry, letting them take her in the same way her imagined blue-water tunnel could take her in. She wants to ask him if he really killed a man, remembering he once told her that killing a man was worse than incest. But she doesn't really want to know. She only wants to let his calm energy seep into her.

"You're out early again this morning," he says.

"I never made it home last night. A forced row to Tiburon on the ebb. I made it."

"My, my," he looks at her with wizened eyes. "You missed your mark, dearest child. You are a true sailor now. Let me give you a hug." He bends into her and she reaches her arms around his neck. Only someone in his eighties could call her a child. She loves him for it.

Russell comes into the café through the front door and walks over toward them.

"Now that's *my* girl, Otto," he says, reaching his long thin arm between them and whispering in her ear. "I miss you, Franny." He pecks her cheek and tells her how worried he's been; how last night after hanging out at the Trieste, he crossed the channel at midnight to find her dinghy missing; how he pulled up to her stern and yelled for her; how he boarded her boat to find an empty bunk; and how he finally put in a call to the Coast Guard.

"Oh, thank you." She can't say more, feeling a blossom of love come up from her heart to her throat and through her nasal passage, spilling into her eyes and down her cheeks. Russell uses his long thin thumb to press the tear away.

"Truth is, I never made it in last night. I slept in the storage unit," she cries. She can feel the oar sticking into her rib.

"Again, my Franny?" Russell says affectionately with curiosity on his brow.

"Again," she says, not really ready to tell him the details.

"She made it through the gale winds," Otto adds.

The three sit together at the corner table. Love wraps around her, and she lets the sweet comfort swirl with chai steaming on her wet face, waiting for the sun to shine on the café's dancing girl logo on the wall, sending its reflection onto the window.

She opens the *Chronicle* to find a discussion about whether to put a suicide barrier on the east side of the Golden Gate Bridge. She reads aloud about the ongoing suicide barricade discussion. "Suicide barrier. We need that inside us, we need a barrier within us," she says.

"We must never do it, Franny. We are sailors and we roll with the punches," Russell adds. He looks toward Otto.

"We are free to decide for ourselves," Otto says. "We were given choice. Each moment we're alive we are choosing between life and death. Ultimately it is our choice."

"What about the ones left behind?" Russell raises his voice. "Isn't it kind of selfish?" He looks toward Franny now.

"We can't be in another person's shoes," she says.

Russell perks up. "What about that suicide barrier, Franny, the one you said we needed inside us? How does that fit in? What about those of us left behind?" he repeats.

"Did I say that? What I mean to say is I can't decide for someone else. Only the dear Lord can know the depths of our souls."

She continues reading, not so sure what she means. She reads aloud the statistical information. "The engineering challenges of adding a barrier fence are immense. A guard rail along the sides of the four thousand two hundred-foot span would interfere with the flow of air through the cables, causing instability to the bridge." She pauses, like a light going off.

"Like us, changing or adding anything can threaten stability. It's all related, isn't it?" she says. She looks deeply into her heart, seeing how her actions have threatened the stability of her sister and Greg's marriage, her vocation, her God, her child's life. All these conditions contribute to her sense of failure. Suddenly she feels a heavy weight on her shoulders, so responsible for her world collapsing.

"What's related, Franny?" Russell asks, putting his face up to hers.

"Not me, I'm a lost soul," Frances says.

"Oh, you're okay, Franny. And I like your soul."

"Thank you," she says but feels a foreboding. Her guilt about the child, Anne and Greg's visit, Anne's letter from India, the cops, the scary sea, and the long night's walk, not to mention her mental confusion, all tip the odds for her. And what about her vows to God not to kill or harm? Do they include killing oneself? How can she promise? But no one is asking her to promise.

Russell sips his coffee. She sees him sitting upright on his elbow, his face close to hers in what looks like adoration, or at least respect. She adores him, and Otto, too. She pours out her heart to them in summary of last night's events as if she were bailing her boat. She rambles on about getting caught in the high winds, making it to Tiburon, only by the grace of God. Then being harassed by the police. Walking the long miles home, sleeping in her storage bin, and being hauled to jail. They encourage her, all ears, especially when she talks of the arrogant pricks, the rude cops, who treat her like a criminal. She doesn't tell them of her despair, though. She wants to keep that to herself and her maker. But it has a way of creeping in even here in the safety of the small café.

The Lady of Sorrow descends upon her. "We're thinly veiled, Russell."

"That's a good one, Franny. I don't know what it means."

"That's a Catholic image, I can see it," Otto offers. "The veil between two worlds, the world of the living and the world of the dead." He looks toward Frances.

"Maybe it's about a bridal veil?" Russell says with a smile.

"Or maybe it's just something that I created in my mind," she says. She wants Russell to understand and stop turning things into a joke. "Don't you see we are between two worlds? God is calling to me."

"I don't hear Him," Russell takes her hand. "I hear tango music."

"I hear Him," says Frances. "He wants me."

"Competition for me, Franny, eh?"

"Who wants you, Frances?" Otto pipes in.

"I want her." Russell looks at her as if she is the most beautiful woman in the world. "It's been two days since I've seen you," he says. "Let's dance."

"I haven't done that in years." She softens.

"Then now's the time."

She listens. Tango music plays on the CD with its staccato beat. She lets the rhythm pulse through her veins. Her feet tap and her legs press into his. He responds to her touch. Russell doesn't move away, but instead meets her, rubbing into her legs and slipping one between them, as they dance a seated tango.

"I'll leave you two lovebirds to play." Otto takes his tea to a table on the other side.

With Russell's touch on her leg, she feels aliveness creeping up her leg to her center. *How can that be after such dark thoughts?* She feels alive enough to dance with this man, to paint Russell into her body.

"You're fidgeting all around, Franny. Does that mean you're getting hot?" Russell asks.

"I'm on fire, Russell. Something is brewing." She slides her hand on his lap.

"Now, Franny, I like that a lot. Let's play, Franny."

"Yes, but I have some work to do first, Russell. This here heat we're making is inspiring me in so many ways." She squeezes his thigh. "But first a pencil?"

Russell takes a small stubby pencil from an inner pocket of his down vest.

She starts to sketch on the paper tablecloth, letting the pencil put her boy in his proper place at the center, with a mother and a father beside him, and around him are the animals—seals and their cubs, a mama whale and her calf, birds sitting on their nest. The scene she draws emerges magically, with the sweet laughing boy at the center, his lips mouthing for more, his feet swinging in the air. Who would remember him if not her? She knows that staying alive matters. *While I'm still here, I'll keep him alive. I'll paint three murals.* She knows for certain that if she leaves this earth before completing the murals, there will be no one to know he existed, no one to see the joy he brought to her for that one year.

"What's with you, Franny? All this energy with so little sleep," Russell says.

"I'm jazzed about some art I plan to do."

"I want to dance with you now, Franny."

Russell and Frances get up and stand in the small space of the doorway, pressed together. Russell caresses her bosom and Frances breathes into Russell's neck, feeling the triangular muscles she loves to watch, marveling at his silky warm skin. He half turns her. She sways with him. He bends her backward, pressing his leg between hers. She feels his hardness. He hugs her and then kisses her mouth hard. They leave the café arm in arm and walk down the street seeing no one but each other.

Russell motors Frances in his skiff to his boat mooring and then puts out the small ladder for her. Once he's in the cockpit he pulls her two hands inviting her in. They make love in the front cabin of the sailboat, rocking and rolling on the floating bed. The sea is gentle after the storm. Frances melts in his strong arms, knowing she's finally done the deed the right way. They fall asleep with their lips pressed together. But not just their lips, they are pressed together from head to toe.

13

Love Letters

"You've been away for three days now," Otto says to Frances when she walks into the chai house early morning, holding a long rolled canvas and a smaller roll of paper.

"Love errands, that's all." She winks at him, placing her materials down.

"You were dancing down the street last time I saw you," he says, opening his sack and taking out a photograph, which he hands to Frances.

LOVE is spelled out in three-inch letters, on 8x10 drawing paper, 140-pound weight. She stares at the hand-drawn letters made with watercolor pencils. "We're on the same page, Otto. This is beautiful. Love is a beautiful thing. Russell and I—we have a special kind of love."

"I'm happy for you," he says, and she can tell he's sincere.

Who knew lovemaking with Russell would be a carefree gentle breeze and not a ferocious storm? She wants to shout about the fullness she feels. But she can't. Not yet. Oh, it isn't guilt that keeps her from shouting out, but something else. What is it? She'd be breaking open, coming apart, she thinks. But certainly she's been carrying some dead weight, like a cemented vault all these years. Does she dare to allow herself this reprieve? If she boasts, won't she lose it?

She sees Otto looking at her lovingly. "Are you here, Frances?" He pats her shoulder.

She appreciates his fatherly gesture, reminding her of Papa Nicola, a tender kind of love she never experienced from her own father.

She looks down and examines Otto's print again. "It's leaves. You sketched this out of autumn leaves."

He describes the scene to her, how he'd been waiting at a bus stop in Mill Valley in the rain and how he'd amused himself by spelling LOVE with the fallen leaves at the curb and then sketching the message with a pencil.

"Clever man. You're an artist, too." He nods.

"If I may ask, what have you been doing for three days, young lady? Honeymooning?"

"Let's just say I was with Russell catching up on life." She winks at him again.

"In the boat?"

"Yes, we spent three glorious days together on the boat. After the storm there was a silvery calm on the bay. The day was so soft, reflecting a satiny gray on the water. Seals bobbed and poked in and out of the bay around the boat. Next day we set sail with me at the helm."

She pauses for a moment, recalling how she and Russell hugged for hours, rolling in and out of each other, then the exuberance of sailing again. She lets the memories seep in. Is this joy she feels? If so, she wants to imprint it on her brain so she can call it forth again and again. But then an old saying comes to mind: *Sailor beware, the calm before the storm.* She looks toward Otto.

"Is the saying the calm after the storm, or the calm before the storm?"

"For you, Frances, the calm came after the storm, though I've heard it said the other way, too."

"Yes, you're right." Frances remembers her ordeal in her small boat. She feels protected by her angels. Nonetheless she gets the willies thinking of another tempest.

"Please don't tell me there is another storm coming my way. I don't think I could make it."

"But you did make it," he reminds her.

"Yes, by the grace of God." Then she tells him how she and Russell set sail around Angel Island on their third day together, and how she raised the main and felt the exhilaration of the sails catching the wind; how they tied up at the public pier at the island and hiked together to the top of Mount Livermore to see the 360-degree view of the bay. Finally, they lunched at Sam's before they retrieved her skiff.

"The miracle is that for those three days, Otto, I felt like I had a normal life." She feels sad about this joyful tryst, recognizing what's uniquely unusual for her may be a common experience for others. How had she waited so long to engage like this? How had life become so hard?

"Always a matter of survival," she says.

"My dear, love is survival, too," Otto says. "Life is adventure."

She caresses his hand.

"It's yours," he says, pressing the sketch into her hand. "An early Valentine's card." He eyes the smaller scroll in her lap. "More drawings?"

"Oh! My project. It's a surprise, but I'll show this sketch to you. I worked on it on Russell's boat, inspired by open time. Just this feeling that I was in the flow of life." She spreads the butcher paper over a table near the window as Otto puts on his bifocals. He gazes at the colorful work on paper, studying each part.

"It's the sketch I started in here the day I was released from jail, after my distress. I colored it in one day on Russell's boat. It's a study for the mural I plan to paint."

"Tell me, who is this boy?"

"That's Nicola."

"Your child?"

She nods.

"That's an old and noble name fit for the czars."

"My grandfather's. You see, he's one of the wise men." She points to her drawing.

"An aristocrat, the way you drew him." He bends into the sketch. "With a thin mustache wearing a tailored suit."

"Hmm! I don't know about aristocrat. But he liked tailored suits. For me, he was a painter," she says, circling Papa Nicola's face with her finger, "my guardian angel, you might say, and I want to have him in the crowd as Nicola's great-grandfather, next to you, Otto." She looks into his soft moist eyes.

"I want to carry this scene onto a large canvas, twelve by sixteen feet, mural size." She looks toward the long canvas roll she found in the dumpster at the shipyard. "I want to reinvent my baby's birth. I want to give him the celebration and welcoming, in communion with the others. I want to give him a normal life with family and children and animals around him." A smile crosses Frances' face. "This is the first of three," she says. "A reinvented nativity scene."

"Grandiose. You're planning an installation."

"Yes, that's it."

"Complete with a cast of recognizable townies," he says, his eyes twinkling. "And animals? You put seals instead of lambs. Wait a minute. That Joseph, I know him." Otto points to the figure. "But from where?"

Frances looks to where he's pointing. It's Greg as the father, holding his son close to him, so that the child is facing outward. Both father and son smile openly for all to see.

"That's your brother. The guy that came in here looking for you."

"Yes, Greg." She has opened the door so that others can see the joyful dyad. "I will put together the pieces. It's right to reunite Anne and Greg, and to give Nicola a Mommy and a Daddy." She declares this even as she wrestles with that familiar feeling that she has done something bad, that she is making up stories.

She jumps to change the subject. "I've got it," she says. "We'll use the back of Paul's studio! He has enough wall space in the loft to hang the three canvases side by side. I'll need about three weeks!"

She considers the last time she saw Paul, who dresses like Santa Claus in the winter and Peter Pan during the rest of the year. John Paul Wayne is a master welder who agreed to weld an iron prow head for the front of her sailboat in exchange for her sanding an old chair he was restoring. Frances had a specific design in mind. She wanted an ornament made of iron designed after a *ferro*, the Venetian symbol on gondolas in the Grand Canal. When his need to compromise on the complicated design took hold, they argued. He never did his share, though she had sanded the chair, even the claw feet. She had no *ferro*.

She resented his entitlement and had kept away from his studio, though she was curious about his works and at times complimented him as they passed one another on the street.

"How are you going to convince him to help? By making him one of the wise men?" Otto asks, interrupting her thoughts.

"Oh, he wouldn't care about that. I have other ways to get his consent." She raises her brows.

"Or get his goat! You're going to make mischief with him, Miss Pia, aren't you?"

"Maybe just that." She smirks as a plan is brewing. "We can pin the raw canvases to the walls in the loft while he works down below. Then I will paint them in acrylic."

"Then you can enter them into the Art Commission winter contest," Otto says.

She raises her eyebrows in interest. "In that case I'll glue each canvas onto a piece of plywood to transport it to the Council Chambers."

"To SFMOMA," Otto corrects.

"That's like shooting for the stars."

"And why not?"

"Let me get the studio first. Can we meet up later? I'd love your help in picking up two more canvases in the city."

"I'll find you, Miss Pia."

•   •   •

She heads down Caledonia toward Paul's studio in the Sausalito shipyard with her small sketch and the large rolled piece of canvas, walking in the direction of the library, wondering what she looks like to others. She looks at the pavement, not wanting to see anyone, especially one of those cops. It hasn't always been this way. She remembers how she and a friend once blithely carried a small sofa from a furniture store in San Francisco to their dorm a mile away, talking and laughing all the way, without self-consciousness. She longs for that feeling of liberation, having tasted it recently when she made love with Russell.

She skips down Bridgeway toward the former shipyard on the waterfront until the pavement gives way to loose gravel surface, where skipping is more difficult. She stops to find her breath, then walks through potholes filled with water from recent rains, reminding her of being a kid again, playing at Blackie's Pasture. Only the shortness of breath tells her she's old. She stops in front of what looks like a large warehouse set back from the water, with windows facing the hillside ridge. The door to Paul's shop is open. She peeks inside.

Paul, looking impishly small, has his back to the doorway. His pointed red hat wobbles from side to side as he whittles a saucer-like bowl the size of an inner tube. He's cutting the wood away from his body so that long thin pieces of slivered wood fly into the underside of a chair that sits upside down on the worktable. She's mesmerized by his rhythmic carving from an enormous redwood burl and stands by quietly, watching the smoothness of his cuts. Then she chuckles, thinking he could sit in it, take it to the slopes, or sail out to sea. Her laughing causes him to stop work and turn.

"Hey, Frances here," she calls out. Paul looks up, surprised to see her.

She enters the warehouse studio space with its two levels and a metal stairway leading to the second floor.

"Wayne!" She calls him by his last name. "I'm here to make a deal with you."

"Oh?"

"I have a project to do over the next few weeks, and I need to use your wall space."

"For a few weeks!" He gulps down air, putting down the knife. "Not another commission, I hope."

"Now don't get your dander up, Wayne. I'm not asking for the ornament for the prow. I just want to paint a few murals and use that wall space." She looks up toward the second story where there's a fully uncluttered, windowless wall. "I'll make it worth your while."

"How's that? Are you propositioning me?" he says, shimmying up close to her and looking at her breasts. His eyes, level with her chest, make her feel uncomfortable.

She pushes him away, the large canvas angling like a spear toward his small chest. He backs off, holding his knife in one hand and using his wooden saucer as a shield. She thinks of Don Quixote.

"This sketch will become an enormous painting for all to see," she says, unrolling the small vividly colored sketch. Remembering Otto's positive response, she wonders if Paul's seeing it will convince him of her merit.

He takes his time looking, studying the sketches she's made. He laughs, pointing at a recognizable shifty city official, standing in the midst of the street folk, wearing his pants below his hips like an adolescent boy. "And there's that Italian restaurateur leading the crowd. What a clown!" Paul says.

"I need your help, Wayne. Please help me."

"Your being here will no doubt disrupt my whole business, the creative flow. Now you can understand that, Frances. You get my drift." He turns away toward the chair, the knife in his hand.

"I'll work upstairs and in the evenings so I won't get in your way," she fires back.

He keeps his back toward her and turns toward the upside-down chair, beginning to whittle. She watches long fine strips of wood fly into the cup of the chair.

"Wayne, you're not going to make me beg, are you?" When he slices more vigorously, avoiding looking at her, she gets closer to his back and whispers into his fuzzy ears, "You know and I know that you've done some despicable things. Remember that time you poured flammables down the sewer by the library?"

Wayne makes out not to hear her, stepping up his pace. "And I remember you were none too kind to that man who used to work for you. You didn't even pay him minimum wage."

Paul stops working, puts down his knife, and brushes the bowl with a soft cloth, removing the fine grains, blowing to dispel the dust, ignoring her accusations.

"Then there were the cats—that litter, you remember those sweet little ones, don't you, Wayne? And that pussy cat that used to come by here with all those Toms. She just up and disappeared, Wayne."

"I was doing her a favor. Damn it! Frances, are you blackmailing me?" He puts down his upholstery cloths and stands facing her. It's a standoff, an old-fashioned duel, their eyes glued to one another's. She watches him examine the drawing and sees his lips change direction to an upward curve.

"This is some piece of work, Frances. The way the street people have some pomp here. I think you might be making a political statement that I subscribe to. Look at the wise men, not the usual. There's Otto."

She knows he's on her side now. Frances looks at her drawing too. The joy she experiences doesn't come from what Paul might see, but from the idea of making it a reality, and doing it right. The act of painting them will set her free.

"Okay, I'll give in only because I want to see the face of the official when he sees how you depicted him with his pants down. He looks like a weasel. Three weeks to get your work pinned on that wall and painted. Then you're out. You got it, Frances?"

"I got it. Thank you. You're kind behind that gruffness."

"Don't push your luck. You don't know when to quit, do you?"

"By the way," she says. "Otto and maybe another helper are gonna be my assistants."

"Pretty soon you'll have all the other vagrants in here, Fran."

"Maybe so." Smiling now, she heads up the metal staircase to the second landing.

"Now you watch your step. I don't want no accidents in here."

She carries the unyielding piece of rolled canvas up the metal staircase.

"You want some help with that?" Wayne yells up.

"Sure do, thank you, again."

He comes on up and faces her.

"Fran, you know you said some pretty mean stuff to me down there. Before we hang this thing, I want an apology."

"You're right to ask that of me." She stops her prepa-rations and faces him. "I'm sorry, Paul." After he cuffs her lightly on her shoulder, they are free to attach the piece of canvas to the wall. He ably holds one side while she pins the opposite corner to the wall with the long narrow metal push-pins she takes from her supply bag.

"You don't have a staple gun we might use, do you?" she asks, as the canvas slips off the wall.

"Now you ask me for one of my precious tools. Next you'll be asking for the moon."

While he's gone for the staple gun, she opens a small notebook and begins to list her gratitudes—making the safe passage across the bay, Russell and Otto, even Paul. But then she feels shame as she reflects on the way she coerced Paul. *Dear God, I have been visited by the devil. May I be humble.*

When Paul returns, she holds the large canvas in place against the wall as he staples the four corners. He gives her the gun for the highest edges. Finished, they stand in front of the blank canvas, staring at the white. The purity of the space reminds her of a snowfield. Before long, she realizes she's in front of the white scape alone. Paul has gone down to the lower room. She listens to the silence, contemplating the unknown, the vast emptiness of space.

As she's readying to leave, Paul presses the key to the side door of the shop into her hand.

"You know how to close those heavy front door pan-els now?"

"Sure do, and thank you." She leaves to walk through the shipyard across Bridgeway to the hardware store, the key tucked in her bra next to her precious ashes, wondering if she is truly up for the task ahead.

• • •

At the store she selects her colors, and then orders six half-gallons of acrylic paint in red, blue, yellow, white, black, and gold. She gathers her supplies, which include brushes and rollers, a rolling pan and extra buckets for mixing colors, and drop cloths. She examines the bill, and sure enough, this stuff costs her this month's security check. She doesn't care about using her money in this way, but wishes she had a patron so she'd have some extra cash for the rest of the month. *How did the great masters manage? Surely Michelangelo worked on commission.*

"Señora, don't forget the masking tape." She turns to face Hernando Iglesio, who's standing beside her at the register. "*Que pasa*, señora?" he asks.

"Hernando Iglesio Cruz, *con mucho gusto*. It's been a while."

"Yes, señora. I think of you often—that day the *jefe* came . . ." She feels heat rise in her face and wonders if he senses her embarrassment.

She changes the subject and asks, "And how is your *abuela*?"

"*Buena*." He looks at the mountains of supplies on the cashier's counter. Frances remembers the warm feeling she had toward him that day, how they spoke of his grandmother's work in the strawberry fields, and the Mexican muralists, too. She felt so joyful on that scaffold, listening to his music, bobbing up and down. Suddenly it occurs to her that she could hire him to help her to move the murals around, glue them to the plywood when they are finished, even paint. When he turns toward her again, she looks into his eyes, dark and fluid. Again an image of his *abuela* floats to mind—she's bent over the strawberries, picking one and then one million. Her hand flutters up to her heart, relating to her hardworking soul.

She whispers to him that she's making a mural of the townspeople.

"If you ever need any help, señora, where I come from in Mexico we produce more than strawberries. We produce great muralists too."

"Like Diego Rivera." Frances will find a way for Hernando to work with her on this project, and more than just plywood-gluing or making frames. She imagines him doing some of the painting, too.

"Can I help you carry this stuff?"

"I'm across the street at the shipyard—a few blocks away?"

"I have time," he says, taking the box of paints and flinging it up onto his shoulder so he has a hand free to carry the shopping bag with the smaller supplies.

They cross Bridgeway, walking at a brisk pace. She tells him of her plans to paint three murals in three weeks. When his eyes widen, she explains her vision for one of the paintings—a new state-of-the-art park that is safe and fun for children, with ponds and birdbaths and a beachfront where dolphins give rides to children.

"I'd like to see that for the kids. Maybe a merry-go-round in the center?"

"Maybe you could help me?" she offers.

"But I need to work full-time, señora."

"I know," she says, wracking her brains. Hiring him might mean going into her inheritance, which she's managed to keep sacrosanct, only wanting to give it to Anne. Oh, if she only had a benefactor or a commission. If she had one, she'd hire him right now, make it worth his while. Maybe Otto will see a solution.

"Tell me, señora, did you paint a mural on the far side of the house a few weeks ago?"

Frances stops. He keeps moving ahead of her, keeping up his brisk pace, still carrying the art materials on his shoulder, until he realizes she's stopped and turns.

"Ah! I've given myself away. You saw the birdbath with the little boy with a bird on his shoulder." She feels sheepish.

"When did you do it? In the dark?" She doesn't answer. "When we found the completed work I couldn't paint over it."

Frances moves up a few steps toward him and reaches out to touch his shoulder.

"And then the *patrón* came home and loved it. And wanted to leave it as a gift for his little girl."

Frances stops at the curb, breathing a sigh of relief. "I can't believe it, Hernando. Someone wants my work."

"And the *patrón* is the mayor of Sausalito, señora."

Imagine that, she thinks.

When they return to the studio, Paul is gone. Hernando carries the supplies up the metal steps and places them near the pinned canvas.

"Muy grande!"

"Not as large as the houses you paint," she says.

"True." He stands in front of the blank white canvas.

"What do you see, Hernando?"

"I see the creation of the world."

"Yes, that is what I want to do. I only wish I could find a way for you to help me."

"*Gracias,* señora. I want that too. You will find me on the corner of Girard and Filbert at my next house." As he walks out, she listens to the way he takes the steps, two at a time. A young strong man in his prime. She feels sad she can't offer him a job. She would love to work beside him. She imagines a scene where they are side by side painting a blue ground on the canvas, with that ghetto blaster playing Mexican songs.

Sitting down in Paul's red upholstered antique chair, she feels her energy expanding down to her feet, then flowing up her back and through the top of her head, through her arms and into her hands. Warm circles of heat flow through her, giving her a more focused attention to aid her in what she must do. She touches the pouch with the ashes and Anne's precious letter, feeling as alive as when she's with Russell.

Before she applies gesso to the canvas, she imagines the transfiguration of the nativity scene as the transfiguration of Nicola's life. She will right the wrongs. She will give him Greg and Anne for parents, and they will love and protect him through his childhood and teenaged years and into adulthood. She will repair the damaged threads of her life cloth.

14

An Act of Confession

The three murals appear in her imagination. The first, the nativity, offers the new world for Nic, Anne, and Greg; in the second, the playground where Nicola died, are pictures of children and their parents, a scene alive with the voices of the innocent facing the promise of joy; in the third, Officer Bentley leads the group of money grubbers, developers, and others who like to rob the city blind. They are heading toward the ferry landing, where a pirate ship awaits them. She pictures a line of them going up the gang-plank for an adventure at sea. She hopes Margaret will get a kick out of this.

Frances spends an easy six hours in front of this first canvas, the sun dropping lower on the horizon. Sketching with charcoal vines, the soft shapes emerge from her drawing hand, as if she is tracing her soft skin with her fingers—the cheeks, the angled nose, the dimpled chin, and the thin body riding off the sides of the canvas. With yellows and reds, her beloved Anne, as the mother in the nativity scene, takes center stage. She pauses, looking at Anne's face, so vibrant and full with her hand lovingly placed on her child's heart. Frances has her standing on an opened half shell like Venus, with Greg beside her, carrying his beloved child, Nic, in one cupped arm with his other around Anne's shoulder. Frances steps back in quiet contemplation before adding the seals and the dolphins as guardian animals, swimming playfully around them.

Frances sighs in relief as she bequeaths Anne the child she never could have. She smiles, thinking if Anne had been his mother Nicola would be alive still. Then come the animals and birds on the canvas: sea mammals, seals, cormorants, pelicans, ravens, and band-tailed pigeons taking flight. As if by magic, the faces of her friends, the wise men and women, appear on the canvas rendered in vibrant colors. The final figure emerges—an older and rounder woman in the upper right hand corner. She's wearing a red coat, riding on the back of a white pelican with its wings outstretched. Her hair is flying in the wind and her smile lights up her face. It looks like she's riding off the side of the canvas.

Frances stares at the magical figure as the light shifts to dusk. When it's very dark, she sits in the chair with the comfy armrests, not moving to turn on the fluorescent lighting but letting the dusk soothe her. She closes her eyes and falls asleep. She awakens to the sound of knocking. It's Otto, carrying some take-out. She smells *rosmarino* and guesses it must be her favorite chicken dish. She rushes down stairs to greet him.

"It's dinnertime," he says. "You're sleeping in the dark."

"I've spent the whole day here in the studio." She looks to the upper level where her work is hung.

"Then I'm glad I brought this for my dear queen of Sausalito," he says, looking at her surprised face. "For us. Some nourishment." He hands her a bag, then he places the warm food on the finishing table in the center of the studio. He produces from inside his coat a bottle of red wine and two wine glasses he's brought from the restaurant.

When they close the doors, they head for the two ancient upholstered chairs and sit down together on the lower floor away from the painting. "Paul should see us now," she says, lighting some candles that sit on the worktable. Otto opens the wine, pours some in each glass, then holds the wine to the light of the candles, swirling it and then putting his nose at the rim.

"Not a Bordeaux," he says, licking his lips. "But dry." They sit a moment listening to the old grandfather clock breathing.

"A toast to the artist," he says. "What kind of artist, Frances? You never said." She looks at him, pausing. He waits, but his eyes like magnets pull her to answer. He won't let her off the hook.

"Let me guess," he says. "You're wildly expressionistic like the swirls and the primary colors that mask the decadence of Weimar Germany… Wassily Kandinski, no, more like Alexej von Jawlensky." Otto's pale face flares, his nostrils widen, and his mouth opens.

"No. That's you, Otto. You're wildly expressionistic."

"Did you ever see the heads of von Jawlensky? The eyes placed diagonally on the face, patches of color, sliced through with black lines?" he asks.

She thinks carefully. "Expressionistic, not really." She pauses in contemplation. "Perhaps some of my portraits look like von Jawlensky's *Mystical Heads*, his *Saviour's Faces*. Ahh, the past," she sighs, a bit saddened by her history, not at all sure she wants to go there.

"You can endure the unendurable," he says. "Look at those German artists, converting the shit of the Nazis to gold. The gift of the darkness. That's the source that drives the art."

"You think?"

She looks into his waiting eyes. She stops. No words, only an awareness that he has seen her pain, or maybe his own. What had Anne said in her last letter about time, or had she imagined it? *Time zooms in all directions until it is the same.*

They sit quietly sipping the faux Bordeaux.

"I draw with leaves in the rain," he says. Was he asking her to speak of her soul? And if so, what would she say? She ponders, thinking how he's encouraging her to open up, to come clean.

She nods. "All I try to do is to make a space in which no one has ever entered. You begin thinking you really know what you're doing, but then you really don't want to know what you're doing. You try things out so you can see and then you wait until something awesome takes over."

"You really don't know what you're doing?" His head bends closer to hers.

She nods. "Then without much effort you're in the zone and you're called to do better," she says, thinking of the flying bird that just appeared on her canvas.

"The zone of surrender," Otto says knowingly. As he says this, her whole body relaxes, even her jaw.

"In that room you feel whole. The room has no walls. It's like the sea. That's what I do." She sits still now, remembering.

"What do you see, Frances?"

"I see a young nun painting religious scenes. There are three paintings."

"These ones you're working on now?"

"No, not these."

She begins to speak freely of the three major works of her life, telling him about the origins of the first painting, a wooden sculpture of a crucifixion at the Basilica of St. Vitale. Since when has her tongue been so loose? Not before these last few weeks, beginning with Greg's visit, then Anne's; not before the bout with the sea; not before the tango with Russell. She wonders at this newly found openness, unavailable to her for decades it seems. Not since she confessed to the priests as a novice. Was it the shame she carries that has kept her so closed? She runs her hands over her chest as if to flick away the soiled feeling that shame imprints. And what of this renewed vulnerability she feels? Otto's looking at her.

"It was of a woman hanging from the cross in Ravenna, Italy. Her name was Eulalia Christiana, and she was hidden away in the cloister—outside and away from the eyes of the parishioners."

Otto raises his eyebrows in seeming interest. "Like you, dear Frances, hidden away in a cloister."

She doesn't let his comment deter her from her story. "Not me, Otto. Eulalia was young and beautiful and nailed to the cross. She, she . . ." Frances pauses and sees that day vividly, as if it were today.

Sister Caterina was extending her hand to Frances as they left the main basilica, with its dazzling mosaics, through a side door into the inner garden. The sun shone bright and warm as she followed the older nun. Frances looked down to see the sister's black orthopedic shoes and short summer white habit. They walked to a far darkened corner where the sculpture hung on a wooden cross.

"Dear God!" Frances gasped, putting her hand over her mouth, the breath seeming to be knocked out of her. "Who is she, a crucified Jesus?"

"*Sì, simile.*" Sister Caterina said, answering her question so simply.

Frances stared at the sculptured figure stuck in the dark corner of the cloister. Like Christ, she was nearly naked. Like Him she had been nailed to the cross with body piercings and a crown of thorns on her head. *Ave Maria*, Frances prayed, her head bowed in reverence to this image. The woman crucified struck a deep sorrow in Frances' heart. One of her breasts, full and round, protruded over the fabric which was torn away. Eulalia's head was bent with her chin resting on her chest.

Sister Caterina told her about the life of the martyred Saint Eulalia, a twelve-year-old girl, who was murdered by the Romans for defying the cruel Diocletian. She was virtuous and prayed to remain in a state of virginity. She was martyred and made a saint.

She could hear the sister praying in front of Eulalia, dropping to her knees in the cloister. "*Miseria, miseria, miseria*, Lord have mercy."

Then the sister told her that the bishops refused to put this piece of art in the main church, that there had been a controversy in the town between the people who were demanding that she be recognized prominently inside the church and those who thought the artwork was sacrilegious. For Frances, the work was sacred sacrilege and must be known.

"She . . . she . . . she . . . was a Christ figure to me, Otto, and I wanted to pull her off the cross right then and there and nurture her wounds, to do CPR. But more, I wanted the world to see her. I didn't want her to be hidden away like the Gospel of Mary Magdalene."

"So you painted her," Otto says.

"I had to paint her."

Otto waits as Frances sits with her own head down. "I had to right the wrongs. Because I had seen her, I had to paint her to honor her. But then I felt I had to show her to the world, all the while knowing why this pose of sensual nakedness was relegated to the back hall. I was fighting. I'm still fighting, Otto. I have to right the wrongs of my life. Don't you see?" She's pleading with him, wanting something he cannot give.

"I can't do it, Frances. I can't right the wrongs for you."

"I know. I've fought with my brush before. And I'll fight again. Maybe this time I can show the world that a mother can give away her dead child to make amends."

"You were going to right the wrongs of the Roman Catholic Church?"

"The Romans, too." She laughs. "I painted her in a small room, the unused larder of our house in Rome. I painted her full size in all her glory. Or maybe she painted me. I painted a full, voluptuous cohort of Jesus Christ, all the while knowing that if I was found . . ." Frances pauses.

"You'd be in deep shit," he says.

"Yes."

"I can almost see her on the mast of the Golden Gate Ferry or hung in a great museum," Otto says. "No more hiding!"

Frances doesn't respond. She is looking beyond now, seeing in her mind's eye the second of her masterpieces—a beautiful, young, alive woman draped over the recently fallen Christ. She is floating over him in her nakedness while a gentle wave caresses and holds them buoyantly together. Her face, serenely sad, lovingly rests on the smooth chest of the dead Christ. The woman is a guardian of the man who has fallen. Mary Magdalene.

Otto and Frances sit side by side in silence. Frances stares ahead at the trees across the way, where a flock of ravens convene in some great mass for the night, but don't sleep; they caw and their sounds penetrate the night and the studio space, maybe echoing the sorrowful scene of the fallen man in the night with the loving woman draped over Him.

"You are far at sea, Frances," Otto says interrupting the silence.

"Yes. I can see her."

She wants Otto to see what she sees, to tell her she was right to paint her like this, so that more people would be able to see her as the one who loved Jesus.

"Your painting of Mary Magdalene was even more controversial than the first," he states, breaking the silence.

She nods, placing her hand on his soft white beard then taking his face in her hands. He allows her to bring his face closer to hers. She whispers, "When I painted her like that, I felt like I was her and she was me; that she was telling me to show the world all the ways a woman could love. I wanted so much to make Christ a more human man."

"Just the way you want the world to see Nicola as an alive boy," he says, grabbing her hands.

"Thank you." They sit as one, face to face.

"Frances, with your paintings you've hit a nerve of the Roman Catholic Church."

"But they expelled me as a Roman Catholic nun."

"RC, royal crap!" says Otto. His eyes bristle.

"And here it is. Am I attempting to go across the grain again? This time to defy the gods? No." She answers her own question. "I'm attempting to repair the world."

"Ah, *Tikkun Olam*, world repair," he says.

"Yes, to set it right through acts of kindness. But for me and for Nicola and for Anne this time. I'm giving him a new life, another chance." She pauses, reflecting on God. "I have forsaken Him, and He has forsaken me. All He ever wanted me to do was . . ." She leaves off the sentence, looking toward Otto to fill in the blanks.

"L-O-V-E," he answers. "Love is ours. The love that is here right now, rather than sequestering it in some forsaken dark corner. You brought it into the room for all to see, Sister Frances." They sit quietly watching the flickering flame.

"And whatever happened to those paintings?" he asks.

"When the Italian Mother Superior found them in the larder, she admonished me. Though I managed to transport them back to San Francisco, they were lost to me."

"Another injustice."

Aloud she says, "Al Sterling, my art teacher and curator, sponsored an art show for Nicola Pia del Aqua at the de Young Museum on December 8."

Otto has a puzzled look on his face. She clarifies, "My grandfather's work will be shown in an exhibit at the de Young Museum in December. Soon. On the Feast of the Immaculate Conception, December 8," she shouts as if he is deaf.

"Soon. In one week's time."

"Yes. Papa painted abstract murals. He took from nature, and then separated the parts."

"Like Picasso," Otto says.

"God forbid. His abstractions are soft and flowing, no

hard edges, more like a Turner, or his teacher's murals of *The Land* and *The Sea*."

"Piazzoni."

"Yes, Gottardo Piazzoni was Papa Nicola's teacher, and Al learned from Papa."

She looks at her watch; it's after midnight. They've circumnavigated the world since dinner and she hasn't even opened the new letter from Anne hidden in her bra. "You can spend the night here if you need to, Otto. And we can catch the noon ferry to San Francisco for those two large pieces of canvas. Unfortunately, art stores are hard to come by in Marin."

"The art store tomorrow, of course." He moves toward an open space, takes the pillows from his chair, stretches out on the floor, and falls asleep.

Frances doesn't move from her chair but sits and reads Anne's letter by candlelight.

15

Word from the Stables

Varanasi India
1 December
Dear Franny,
Since I saw you in Sausalito a month ago powerful
dreams and images come to me. I wish I could tell
you all about them. You are so good with dreams.
Ahh, but then my hand would get cramped. HAHA!

Frances feels her own hand twitching and puts it on her chest, praying *mea culpa,* beating her chest three times. *Have mercy on me, dear Lord.* She feels a bit of fear, a little catch in her throat, not wanting and at the same time, wanting to know what Anne has to say. She looks over at Otto sleeping on the studio floor, sending a whispering breath from his nostrils. She reads on though her eyes drift back and forth, rocking her from side to side with sleepiness. She blinks against nodding off.

Yesterday as I walked along the embankment I caught a glimpse of a woman in a red sari. I swear it was you, Franny. I stopped, looking, searching, drawing nearer to her. Frances, was that you bathing with your clothes on?

Frances feels confused, and says in a whisper, "No, I'm here in Paul's studio in front of a painting of you." It occurs to her that perhaps she and Anne are seeing each other through some weird telescoping of time. She pats her chest again. She wishes she were nearer to Anne to reassure her, to hug her, to put her at ease, to tell her not to worry. Of course, she didn't have to shower with her clothes on. They were not that prudish. As soon as she thinks this, a pang of remorse swats her; she remembers what she did with Greg, feeling regret. How simple it might have been if she had been the woman bathing in the Ganges, where they cremate their dead.

I'm haunted by Daddy's death. Oh how I wanted to wake him up. Remember how I even tried to open the lid of his metal coffin? It was you who gently lifted me out, Franny. Remember that old game we played about the hen? The hen who saved the little goose. It was you who helped me talk again.

Frances shivers, pulling her red coat over her shoulders, looking over at Otto stretched out on the mats in the studio, but she sees her cold-faced daddy laid out in a blue suit in a satin lined casket. Then she sees Anne climbing up and onto his cold hands.

Frances sits there in her chair, tapping out the beat to the old poem she once taught to Anne, mouthing the words.

One day, upon a time, long ago, they grew a love between them, no matter who could see the hen was not the mother.

She sings the lyric as a lullaby until her eyes become heavy and close. She's asleep before she reads the last line of Anne's letter.

16

Born to Cry

When Frances wakes up, she's still sitting in the studio with the onion-skinned letter on her lap, which she neatly folds. All is quiet in the loft. Otto has replaced the cushions and left the studio. She looks at her watch. Still enough time to make the noon ferry to the San Francisco art store to buy the large canvases. She gathers her stuff, carefully putting the letter into her bra next to the ashes.

As she runs the familiar route to the ferry landing, time is shifting forward and backward like some movie from the forties, where she sees herself running toward the waiting ship where Otto's waving to her from the upper deck. But wait, she can't catch up because she's running backward in time as well, seeing the mute nine-year-old Anne and the house in Tiburon, dark with the shades drawn. Anne was rocking in a little chair with an upholstered seat and arms. Quiet, except for Mama's deep sighs that screamed out loud of her despair. Low tones like a dirge alternated with her moaning, goading for Anne to speak. The rooms, hollow and empty, appeared different from Frances' school where girls ran around, eager to inhale life.

Frances feels chills as she runs up the gangplank and onto the ferry, shaking this memory away.

"Otto asked the captain to hold the ferry for you," says the ticket man.

"He has a way, doesn't he?" Frances says, easing herself onboard toward the upper deck.

"We'll make up the time when we're out of the channel!" the attendant yells behind her.

Frances walks the stairs to the upper deck where Otto greets her and takes her arm, pulling her toward the seat he has saved under an overhead heater. They sit silently, side by side as the boat pulls away from their hill town. A gull hovers in the updraft at the stern. Otto pulls the collar of his tweed woolen jacket close at the neck. Then he unfolds a scarf from his pocket and offers it to Frances, who is sitting in prayer, her lips whispering, "Lord, You are merciful . . ."

A gull stills above her head now. She stops to watch.

"The stuff we're buying will be heavy, Otto, not like that bird."

"Yes, this is so," he says.

She prays, the Saint Francis prayer, *O, Divine Master, grant that I may not so much seek to be consoled as to console; to be understood as to understand; to be loved as to love . . .*

"Maybe that gull was Nic. Do you believe that the dead are with God?" Frances asks.

"That I cannot say."

"More and more I have communion with Nicola," she confides.

"Ah, Nicola."

"You know my grandfather died when I was a child and then my Nicola died when he was an infant. And my father died when Anne needed him most. Is there some meaning to all this suffering?"

"Ah, dear friend, you ask of the great mystery."

"I don't know why Nic was taken from me, nor do I understand why he was given to me."

"There are no answers, only questions." He squeezes her hand.

"*Sunt lacrimae rerum*," she quotes from the *Aeneid*.

"Isn't that our burden, to feel the sorrow? We are humans," Otto asks.

Frances sits motionless next to her friend. Her eyes are narrow. Tears rise into the corners, filling them. She sees herself as the Sorrowful Virgin, cradling her purse like a child close to her heart space, one palm face-up holding his bottom, and the other palm resting on his heart. Like that, she rocks the imagined child. Is it her sister or the dead boy she comforts in that little rocker of her hands? As the waves rock her soul, she lets the heavy weight she feels drop her chin. Tears slide down her cheeks, a refreshing moisture on her skin.

"Yes, yes. Cry, Frances, cry," Otto says lovingly. "Cry more than less."

They sit on the top deck, an odd pair in concert.

"Have you heard about the sin eaters?" Frances asks, regaining composure. Without looking at him, still holding the child in her mind, she tells Otto of a myth she'd heard. "They were a sect of people whose fate was to eat the sins of others. After someone died they were called upon to sit with the deceased. They participated in ritual magic to absolve the sins of the dead. Or maybe they lived in Dante's *Inferno*," she says.

"Maybe they lived anchor out," Otto says, a twinkle in his eye.

"Maybe my calling is to eat the sins of the world." She turns to face her friend.

"And what would you do with with those sins?"

"I'd go to the water's edge where everything is thinly veiled and purify myself. But when I could not, I'd go to the edge of insanity." She thinks of the woman in the sari bathing at the water's edge, and hears Anne's voice, *Is that you, Franny?* Frances puts her face in her hands and lets out deep sobs like the ones her mama used to make and knows now how her mama felt. This is Mama's despair she's eaten.

"Maybe your tears come to wash away the stains," Otto says.

"That's poof! The wounds are always there. I was born to cry."

"Is that true, or is it an opera, Frances?"

"It's an aria from *Giulio Cesare in Egitto*. I took those arias to heart."

"You ate them."

"After my child died, I had my pain and that was all I had. Sometimes you cling to what is palpable." She looks to the sea. "Ash to ash," she says, touching her breasts where the child's fine ashes sit next to Anne's letters.

"Ashes to ashes. We are particles that will return to the Great Mother for another passing," she says. Just then the clock on the tower of the ferry building rings the half hour. It's past noon. The boat pulls into the dock at the ferry building. Otto places an old cotton hanky in her hands.

"Do you want to stay on board and head home?"

"No. We have an errand to do." She gets up.

He takes her hand as they walk slowly down the metal steps to the lower landing, heading for a bench where a little boy chases a pigeon. People sit with picnic lunches facing the water. Frances and Otto hold hands in the midst of the festivities. Frances wipes her nose.

"Let's sit a moment," he says. They take a bench in front of the ferry building and stare at the boats and the passersby.

"On *El Dia de los Muertos,* Mexicans welcome the spirits home and then dismiss them," he says.

"No, I haven't freed them in that way, if that's what you're asking me to do," Frances says. "If I dismiss the boy, I would be a lost soul. I have a harsh God living inside of me."

"Then, it's the harsh God you should dismiss to make room for a forgiving God."

She looks up at her wise friend. "I have not forgiven God for the suffering He has given me." Then she prays aloud. "Oh, dear Lord, how have I forgotten Your love for the wretched me."

A deep sense of calm like the fine sand in an hourglass washes through her body.

They walk toward the Embarcadero holding hands, crossing over toward Market Street to join the crowds of people as they push through the wind tunnel created by the skyscrapers. With the sunlight obscured, they walk briskly as if pushing an unyielding wall. Eventually they take a left onto Second Street and walk toward the art store.

•   •   •

An hour later, toting their purchases—two large pieces of canvas, seventy-two inches wide by twelve feet long, and a gallon of gesso—they head back to the ferry, managing the weight of the materials awkwardly with the wind behind them, propelling them forward. The gallon of gesso pulls down on Otto's joints so his arms look so long. Frances imagines how that must hurt his old joints. She feels the roll of canvas resting diagonally across her bosom. She must look as though she is stuck to the long part of a cross, like Him carrying His burden.

"Mission accomplished." Otto takes a seat on the sky deck of the ferry.

"Help me, Otto." She sits beside him.

She tells Otto about her wish list—to have a patron to help her to complete the mural. That she wants to offer Hernando, the house painter, some cash to help her finish in a week's time. She's eager to let Nic go by giving him renewed life in her paintings—to free herself from this obsession.

"Otto, you are such a good friend and here I go wanting more. Maybe you could be my patron?" she jests, rolling her eyes up into her head. His eyes widen and he smiles.

"I can!" Otto laughs.

Frances' mouth falls open. "How can you afford that?" She takes his hand and cups it in her lap.

"I'm a pensioner. I once had a radio station."

Frances laughs and laughs with Otto and then their laughter expands as gulls swoop before them in some kind of wonder. She imagines him as a kind Mr. Rogers, soothing the hearts and souls of his children or playing Beethoven sonatas for his listeners.

17

The Feast of the Immaculate Conception, December 8

Frances catches up with Hernando at his new site, a corner house on Turney Street where he's sanding old paint. She stops to watch him prep the white house before calling to him. When he hears her voice, he turns and smiles then jumps off the porch.

"Señora, you don't want to paint here," he says.

"No, I came to offer you a job helping me with the murals. I have the money now."

He looks at her, seeming surprised. "Can you help me?"

"Sí, I can paint with you in the evenings and on Saturday."

"Tonight?" she asks.

When he nods, she tells him that she plans to paint through the next week of days and nights. They make a plan for him to come to the studio after work to begin painting the murals.

• • •

"You have a good eye," she tells him as he sketches fluidly on the second mural, detailing the carousel at the playground and the slide. He tells her that as a child he drew everything he saw and now he draws with his two boys.

On the seventh day of their work together, Frances wakes to the early light and the sound of neighborhood cats prowling on the rooftop. She becomes alert to their cries. The crescendo of the screeching cries—*Meow, meeooow, meeeooow*—borders on pain in her ears. She feels an ache in her heart for them. Their cries remind her of an infant in distress, or of her own sounds when she's on night patrol. *Where am I?* she wonders. *Not in my boat. Not in Malik's Olds. Not in jail.* Her arms rest on the red upholstered chair. She sees her bare arms splattered with paint. When the cats meow again, she's dreaming of the coming of the Christ child, for this is the Advent of the Christmas season. Only the harmonica riff of the cats on the metal roof assures her she's still alive. They prowl and drape themselves along the gutters of the tin studio in some strange connection to her. *And where is Anne? Still in India,* she recalls.

As she prays for Anne's safe return home, she remembers this is the day, December 8, of the preview of Papa Nicola's paintings. She taps the top of her head, as if to get the time set in there, and then surveys her mural paintings. Here in all its glory hangs the completed six-foot mural nativity scene with beautiful Anne holding the baby. It's the Anne she has recently seen at the pier, elegantly aged and smiling. She moves her eyes toward the two other canvases whose blue backgrounds, painted by Hernando, remind her of their painting together last night. The canvases offer her a serene and peaceful vastness on which to tell her stories. She likes the idea that she is telling stories in her paintings, stories that are calling to be born. But she must put their completion aside to make Papa Nicola's preview.

Frances cleans up the paints and the brushes and leaves the studio through the side door, walking the half-mile along the docks to her storage locker near the public restroom to gather fresh clothes. In the restroom, she marvels that she has some proper tweed to wear. She pats down her hair and freshens her face, then walks to the bus stop across the street and waits for the Golden Gate Transit to San Francisco. When she realizes she's missed the bus, she starts walking up Bridgeway, holding out her thumb.

At Alexander Avenue a woman in a red Saab pulls over. "Are you going to San Francisco?"

"Yes, I just missed the bus."

"Get in," says the middle-aged woman.

"I don't usually hitchhike," says Frances, "but the buses only come every hour or so on weekends. You're a lifesaver!" She looks at the woman. Her eyes are visibly puffy.

"And I don't usually pick up strangers either," says the woman. She pauses, swallowing hard. "But today . . . I've just been diagnosed with breast cancer." Tears fill her eyes.

"Oh, dear one," Frances buckles forward as if she, too, were struck with a poisoned arrow. Frances herself feels like the martyred Saint Sebastian. When she looks up, the woman is crying.

"Let's pull over up ahead so you can cry." Frances feels herself weakened by the driver's news and imagines they are soul mates. The woman pulls over and the two of them sit quietly on the side of the road as cars whizz by toward the Golden Gate Bridge.

"My name is Frances."

"Gail," says the crying woman. "I'm still in shock. I don't mean to sob to a perfect stranger."

"Please. We are sisters on the road," Frances tells her. "Cry if that's what's here for you. Tears are cleansing to the soul." Is she's talking to her own soul or do those words come from Otto?

"Thank you." Gail sobs, then tells Frances that she just moved here from Southern Maine to be near her son and his family, that they're very supportive. Frances feels a flick of envy that Gail has a son who will take care of her. She again mourns that she has no son, this pain her constant companion. Although she wants to console Gail in her troubles, she is once again self-absorbed and feels ashamed by it, *For it is in the consoling that we are consoled,* she prays to St. Francis.

"I lost my home in Maine to fire. A nightmare. And then I receive this news," Gail says.

Frances keeps her hand on Gail's. The woman sighs, seeming to regroup. She puts the car into drive.

She turns to look at Frances before pulling into traffic. They look at each other's hands, stuck together in an *elixir of love.* Frances remembers she has the white hanky Otto gave her in her skirt pocket, but she doesn't want to move.

"You're kind," Gail says, her swollen eyes now dry.

"You, too," Frances says, now reaching for the hanky.

When Gail adjusts herself, she enters into the flow of traffic on Alexander Avenue, heading toward the Golden Gate Bridge. "Where are you going anyway? I forgot to ask."

"I'm going to the de Young Museum to see some murals."

"I'll take you there."

Frances starts to object but stops herself. She will accept this ride from her new friend.

"Are you an artist?" Gail asks.

"Yes, but the artist at the museum is my granddaddy. I'm going to see a preview show."

"Ah, granddaddies are special."

"His life was my saving grace. If only . . ." She stops.

"If only he could see you now, and know how kind you turned out," says Gail.

As Frances bends in toward Gail's face she smells her lavender, surprised she hasn't noticed it before. She nods as they approach the bridge, sailing across the span and onto Park Presidio.

When they reach the park, Frances directs Gail to the passenger drop off in front of the main door. Then she thanks her for the ride and says goodbye. As Gail pulls out into the stream of cars, Frances watches her drive away, feeling cleansed by their experience.

• • •

I'll be sure to add her presence to my mural. Our Father, Who art in heaven, she prays, looking up at a seagull as if it were God, *hallowed be Thy name. Thy kingdom come, Thy will be done. I know You are here with me and since the day I was born. May You watch over Gail in her time of agony in the garden.* She wraps herself in her arms against the chilled air, cherishing her God's company.

She turns into the newly built de Young Museum, following the fault line created on the paved entryway to the museum by Andy Goldsworthy. Then she pays the entrance fee, confirming with the attendant the location of the Pia del Aqua exhibit and heads straight for the Piazzoni Murals

Room, where her grandfather's work is hung. Frances has been in this room before to see the murals created by her grandfather's beloved teacher, Gottardo Piazzoni, who was commissioned to paint a suite that would embrace the East and the West and celebrate the Pacific Rim. Designed for the old San Francisco Library, the ten panels rested there until they were carefully transferred to the de Young. *Strange how Papa Nicola's work will be next to his teacher's. He would roll over just as the dear Lord rolled over in his tomb. May they rest in peace in a sky room devoted to both of them.*

Frances enters the great hall just off the interior courtyard, the Piazzoni Mural Room, a sanctuary for Frances. She stands spellbound between Piazzoni's two suites of ten murals, called *The Land* and *The Sea,* each twelve-by-six feet in dimension, ten of them, and wanders to the center of the great room without even seeing her grandfather's masterpieces at the far end of the hall. She freezes in the center, staring at the five murals called *The Sea,* marveling at their simple beauty, their call to the horizon, their vision. They take her breath away while at the same time breathing life into her. The elemental beauty touches her soul. Wrapped in stillness, she stands before the great land and seascapes with every cell in her body vibrating, her knees shaking and her eyes filling with emotion.

She remembers once her knees trembling, her heart beating like a drum, bringing her to the floor the first time she saw a whole room filled with the enormous canvases of Jackson Pollock at NY MoMA. She had a similar reaction to the El Grecos at the Legion of Honor, Piero Della Francesca in Arezzo, Murandi in Bologna, Bellini in Venice. All of her favorite artists enter into her soul, leaving her quaking open in the middle of this gallery.

She stares longer and deeper, letting the art bring her close to the divine, giving her a vast and boundless feeling of eternity. She doesn't know for how long she stands here in the middle of the great room with its newly installed wooden floors and Payne's gray paint. She doesn't know if others are in the gallery. All she knows is that she's in a cathedral and God is here with her. Filled with *The Sea*, she spins around 180 degrees to view *The Land*.

Equally exquisite are five panels of the California hills, golden and serene, inviting her to feel the heat rising from the earth on a summer's day, the world Piazzoni has created. The peacefulness of the natural scene enfolds her. A lone horseman on the first panel anchors her in her own body. She listens to her heart sing, not noticing a large group converging on the center of the room, clinging in a tight circle to a museum docent. Frances instinctively backs up, but stops feeling a warmth of closeness. She half turns to find a woman standing near her. She looks down and stares at the woman's shoes, which conform to narrow feet. Smooth, tight, black leather shoes hold what Frances imagines to be dancer's toes and narrow heels.

A special fit that Mama had to order, a double or triple-A heel. As she follows the curvature of the shoes, she sees a bulge on the inner side before the big toe. She feels pain for the woman in the tight shoes. Her own knees twitch the way they did in front of *The Sea* moments earlier. She wants nothing more than to soothe those feet, to anoint them, to wash them the way Mary Magdalene washed Jesus' feet. She doesn't let herself fall to her knees to do the blessing, but holds the feeling as the woman in the tightly fitting shoes turns toward her.

She looks up. It's Anne. Frances is shocked. She stares at her, taking in her short, stylishly cut hair, streaked with strands of silver threads, the casual skirt and matching suit jacket. Frances fidgets from foot to foot. The women gaze at each other and neither moves. They stand in silence. Separate and together. Frances peers deeply into Anne's eyes. They are her father's eyes and the chiseled nose belongs to Papa Nicola. Then Frances registers the surprised face of her beloved sister Anne, who is here, standing beside her and not in India. She feels the tension, an excitement. Her heart races and she imagines her face is flushed.

She pauses, then says, "Your nose, you have a stud."

"A piercing," Anne says, tilting her head up, lifting her hair to expose her ear where other similar studs climb.

"Did it hurt?"

"No," she says, reaching out to touch Frances hair. "Your hair is platinum now with red strands and still so soft. I hadn't noticed your hair that day on the pier. You wore a blue kerchief."

"And you have a few silver threads," Frances says, reaching her fingers up toward Anne's face. "Remember Mama used to bleach hers blonde."

"And that big bouffant she wore," Anne says.

"All teased like a rat's nest."

"Mama never washed it."

"You're wearing Mama's wedding ring. Where is yours?"

"In a drawer for a while," Anne says, diverting her gaze to the space between *The Land* and *The Sea*. "Frances, look. On the far side of the room above the windows where the docent is pointing."

"I can't take my eyes off you," she says.

"Papa's show. Franny, look."

"You're home." Frances wants only to look into Anne's eyes, behind her eyes. She hasn't yet seen her Papa's paintings, which hang on the far side of the great public room. They stand enfolded by the art while their hearts beat as one.

Then she hears a woman's voice. "The work was recently retrieved from some dark chamber where it rested, entombed away from view."

Frances thinks the woman is describing Anne and Frances, who, it seems to her, have been entombed. Papa's murals have pulled them into the same sphere above the ground.

A crowd of people led by a beautifully dressed docent gathers near them. "Here, amidst the admirable calm of a master's vision of limitless nature, abstracted to its essence, universal and specific to California, we find the current show of two more Bay Area artists whose work was recently rescued by San Francisco artist Al Sterling."

"Rescued?" a man from the small group of art patrons asks.

"Yes, the works of both these artists were in storage away from view. In addition to Nicola Pia del Aqua, we have the work of his granddaughter, Frances Margaret Pia."

Frances hears the docent's words but they don't register. She walks toward the works of her grandfather, dazzled by their subtle beauty, but as she follows along the installation from the right, there she sees her own work alongside his. She stands in awe before her lost works. They are so familiar and yet they are newly born, like the resurrected Christ. They have been raised before her eyes.

First she sees the beautiful Eulalia Christiana hanging from the cross. As Frances stares in adoration, it seems that Saint Eulalia's eyes twinkle while her breast seems to pulse, just as her own heart beats wildly; Eulalia's lips, pursed in a gentle smile of knowing, wears a crown of roses just as Frances imagines for herself on this day of joy. Frances stays united to the female Christ and to the crowd with Anne beside her, squeezing her arm the way she used to as a child, but then Frances is called to the middle painting of the loving young woman draped over the recently crucified man. The painting shines with the passion of familial and erotic love and the humility of life's sorrows and joys. Frances stays with the work, admiring the grace she finds in the lines with their serpentine quality, but she doesn't feel she owns the body of work. The work is for the others. She does not claim it as her own. It does not belong to her.

She hears the docent explaining, "The three paintings, both sacred and political, were recently discovered in the archives of the San Francisco Archdiocese. Painted by Ms. Frances Pia when she belonged to the Order of the Sacred Heart. The artist painted in secret in the 1980s as a practicing nun and art historian. A millennium painter, a millennium subject," says the docent.

The crowd envelops Frances as they gaze at the works of art, none of them aware that she's the artist. They whisper to each other like the gossipers pictured in old story paintings. "A Catholic nun painted these," one says. Frances thinks to herself that not much has changed, yet she knows everything has changed.

Finally, Frances walks toward the last painting, her triumph. Patrons of the museum stand glued to the female apostles who toast their wisdom teacher at the last supper. The viewers also raise a hand with Mary, seeming to toast these magnificent women apostles who stand tall near their beloved teacher. Mary Magdalene has the spotlight, with a beam of light shining on her raised hand as she holds the golden chalice as a toast of love for their beloved Christ and teacher.

They move away from the crowd toward their papa's work. As tears of joy come to Frances' eyes, Anne whispers, "Franny, Papa would be so proud to know the two of you hang together at the de Young."

"Hang," Frances' lips part in a smile. Then she laughs out loud.

"Yeah, he'd have fallen off that ladder," Anne says.

"I remember you as a toddler. He'd lift you up there so that you could be taller than the rest of us, sitting with a paint brush in your hand."

"I guess he did let me do a dab here and there, but my gifts come from Nonna in the kitchen. Wouldn't Papa Nicola love to be here among the Piazzoni and the Pia del Aqua at the de Young?" Anne says.

"And have a dish of that fabulous pasta you make. He is here beside us, Anne. Don't you think?"

"I guess." They stand in the presence of something glorious. Then Frances faces Anne. "You must have something to do with bringing this art together. You knew about his art, but mine? However did you find it?"

Anne squirms before speaking as if she is choosing her words. "Before Al died," she begins, "he contacted me as the executor of Papa's estate, saying he'd like to have a show. Of course, I knew where Pa's last show had been held and where his paintings were stored. When I contacted the Mission Gallery they easily released these works."

"But mine. I'd sent mine to the Mission Gallery. How?"

"I'm not sure. Al asked me if he might add a few of your

works. To my surprise, he told me you had painted in his art class but he had lost touch with you."

"Yes, I went to his class after I ran away from your house," Frances says, "but these three paintings were ones I painted in Italy and then lost track of them. How did you find them?" She feels incredibly exposed relating these long-hidden details, which seem like cobwebs in her mind. But then it seems like yesterday, moments that need to be told now.

"Sister Mary?" Frances beams. Mary had been the keeper of her whereabouts and her saving grace during those months when she was pregnant and without a home.

"Yes, Sister Mary knew where your paintings were stored. You had told her. When they had been confiscated by the Archbishop before you left the order, Mary had filed a petition on your behalf to store them in your absence. When I saw them, I finally knew why you had to leave your order."

"Yes, yes," Frances says.

"I authorized them for this exhibit as a gift to you, Franny."

For a minute they reenter the same universe in which they are sisters united by a loving grandfather, father, and mother. For a moment the battle between them dissolves, the betrayal and the agony is forgotten.

"Anne, please forgive me for what I did."

"Franny, I forgive you for what happened between you and Greg as much as I can." They stand face to face, staring at each other for some eternity, their eyes seeing and maybe even speaking. Then Anne turns away, maybe in discomfort, but turns again toward Frances. "Franny, I know about your loss, about your baby's death. Greg told me when I first returned from India. I'm so sorry."

"Thank you," she says, biting her lower lip.

"I wasn't there for you when he died in the way you were there for me when Dad died. I can't imagine what it's like to lose a child."

Frances takes Anne's hand and presses it to her heart. Then sees an iridescent lime band around her wrist. What is she seeing? A dazzling dragon? No. She stares, fingering each design in the chain of green tattoos which reflect luminous iridescent light next to Anne's tanned skin. What she sees is a tattooed bracelet.

"I did it with my Indian family, Sanjay and Sangeeta, before leaving Varanasi."

Frances stares, examining the dazzling psychedelic images. A parade of green goslings follow in the same direction as an old red mother hen.

"It's the story about the hen who, when she lost her own babies, sat on the abandoned nest of goose eggs until they hatched, the way you once waited for me to come to."

Frances is filled with the kind of joy that brings up tears. "I've missed you, Anne, you don't know how much." Frances clutches her heart, feeling like a kid in love.

They linger, both together and separate, for many moments, holding hands until they are lost in the commotion of the show. The crowd surrounds them, swallowing them and then coming between them. Frances loses grip of Anne's hand and doesn't know which way to turn, whether to grab Anne and hold her tight, as a feeling of panic rushes into the space where her joy had resided. She wants to run, to leave the museum through the fault line as described by Andy Goldsworthy, never to return, to be swallowed up in the opening of the earth. The lightness of forgiveness she felt moments ago is pushed out by a rush of panic, rendering her paralyzed. She feels dizzy and can only think of getting away to the restroom. But how? The crowd is suffocating her, leaving hardly a space to move. Anne is no longer at her back, but is encompassed by the family of Al Sterling, who open their arms to her, maybe thanking her for helping to make all this happen. Frances is desperate now. She can't stand the crowds.

Will I ever see Anne again? loops in her mind. Their reunion was too short, but she pushes her way out of the crowd and finds the exit. She leaves the Piazzoni Mural Room without turning back.

18

Christmas Eve

Anne's visit to Paul Wayne's studio coincides with Advent, the time for the coming of the child, the time for new light. Frances and Anne sit together facing the finished murals. Frances still can't believe Anne accepted her invitation to celebrate Christmas Eve with her. Candles flicker on the workbench. Frances stares at the Mary figure in the mural and then at her sister, who sits in the blue chair beside her. Anne is still as radiant as ever, but a bit more radical now with the nose piercing. Frances is pleased with how she painted Anne and decides she won't add piercings to the mural.

They sit quietly in adoration, their breath mingling as one, giving a soft waft of air to the flickering light. *Was this how they awaited the Christ child?* The rain has stopped and the sun has set. Frances' stomach gurgles, reminding her she hasn't eaten all day.

"You're hungry, Franny."

"Yes, but sitting with you like this fills my spirits."

"You are so funny," her sister says.

"I put on the finishing touches today for you."

"I see you included yourself as one of wise *women*. And there's Papa and Al too. And who is that bearded man?"

"That's my patron, Otto, holding balloons."

"Frances, you have me holding the baby. Is that Nicola?" Anne's voice holds a tender surprise.

"I have given him to you and Greg." She looks toward Anne, who has a startled look on her face, so different from the playful one she has painted on the canvas.

"Franny, why didn't you put yourself there?"

Frances takes a moment and looks intently at the painting as if it will give her the answer. She focuses on the animals and the other children who seem to protect the space. She names one by one the faces of the children she knows from the library park – Isabella, Milla, Ella, Brigette, Daisy . . .

"Franny." Anne's voice pulls her to the moment. "Why have you given me your child?"

"I wanted you to have him. He belongs to you," Frances says, matter-of-factly.

"Oh, Franny. He will always be your child."

They are interrupted by a knock on the door.

"Franny," comes a man's voice.

It's Russell. She goes down to let him into the studio. "Food service, Franny," he says on the other side of the door. She opens the door.

"I've missed you these days on the docks," Russell says. "Hungry for you. It's been a week," he whispers, pecking her cheek. He carries piping hot food: spicy veggie stew, chapati, hot steaming chai, cups for wine. He follows her to the upper level where Anne sits before the painting. Frances sits next to

Anne, feeling some tension from their interrupted conversation. Or was it finished?

He puts the food on the worktable and pulls a folding chair to sit next to the two sisters, sitting in the antique upholstered chairs. They all face the recently created murals, looking together at the scenes.

"Who is the woman in the painting? Is that your sister?" Russell studies the Mary and the woman sitting beside him.

"Younger than me," Frances says. "My baby sister is fifty-three years old now." She looks toward Anne.

"She's a lovely woman, like you." He pours some wine into three Styrofoam cups. Frances takes the wine he offers.

"I've missed the last fourteen years of your life," Frances says, handing Anne a cup of red wine. Anne accepts and then places a gentle kiss on Frances' forehead.

"Anne, this is my beau, Russell. He takes good care of me." They smile at each other.

"Franny, I love that you put your own face among the wise. And look!" He points to the far right hand corner of the painting. "You are the woman on the giant bird flying off the canvas," Russell comments, taking up his wine.

"I fell from heaven in her eyes and she has forgiven me," Frances says, looking toward Anne who sips the wine.

"Thank God," Russell says.

"She forgives me for what I've done." Frances finishes his sentence.

"No, that you fell from heaven. That's no place for a woman like you."

"Maybe. But, God gave me a baby, a son."

"Look at me, Franny."

She looks into the joyful eyes of the man who lives on

the sea, the man who makes love to her, the man who does a not-so-bad tango.

"And you gave him back, Franny."

"God made a mistake. Nic was meant for her." She looks at the mural with Anne carrying the infant and then at Anne.

"God's mistake."

"God's mistake. I forgive him his mistake and mine," she says.

They look at a golden light reflecting on the trinity, baby Nicola held in the hands of Anne and Greg. "As it should be, once and for all," Frances manages to say.

"Let's toast that, Franny," Russell reaches toward their cups. Anne toasts with them, but then excuses herself and quietly walks down the steps. They hear the door close gently.

Frances feels unsettled by Anne's leaving, thinking too much talking has pushed her away, worrying that Anne is mad or sad.

When Russell takes Frances cheeks in his hands and pulls her face into his own, she forgets. He holds her, inhales, his nose like a bunny twitching for her. She smells his rough scent, a mingling of sea weed and the waxes he uses to coat the boats, the heavy red wine, and that other scent, a musky odor that has her shouting, "Hooray! Hooray!" Her exuberant outburst echoes against the metal roof of the warehouse studio, shouts that call out to the world, to the people of Sausalito, to *The Land* and *The Sea*, to the cats on prowl, to her Russell.

"Now that's my Franny," he says, bringing her lips to his, licking them, licking her nose and cheeks and eyebrows.

"Want to dance?" asks Russell, as he hums some bars from the tango music.

He takes her in his arms and they dance in front of the mural until she feels dizzy.

"Look at that! What do you want to tell your baby, Franny?"

"Merry Christmas, child of mystery." Frances sings softly over and over in all the languages she knows. "*Feliz Navidad, Joyeux Noël, Buone Natale, caro bambino.*" Then she and Russell sing, "Silent night, holy night, all is calm all is bright." Their sweet voices fill the large room, resonating against the walls and the old furniture, sending colored ribbons of sound throughout the studio, crisscrossing the room, reaching the children. Frances imagines Nicola pulling the red ribbon and Milla the blue one, Isabella attaching to the orange one. She pictures them dancing around, pulling the sky ribbons, spinning and twirling, laughing and singing. They're all of one living world.

"Hello in there," a woman's voice calls. "Sausalito Police."

"Come in, come in, Officer Bentley."

"I saw the lights on and wanted to wish you a merry Christmas."

"Yes, join us. We are singing. It's Christmas Eve," Russell says.

"Oh, I remembered this is your studio for the month. Am I interrupting?"

"Please come in, Officer Bentley." Frances looks over the upper railing at the smart young policewoman, inviting her in. She enters through the small side door, makes the stairs to the upper level, and fastens her eyes onto the scene portrayed in the large mural which is illumined by the golden spotlight. First focusing on the left side, Officer Bentley then moves her eyes to the center and right, landing on a large group of people.

"Oh, my!" she exclaims.

"Yes, there you are!" Frances says, her lips parted in a

wide smile. Another knock. Otto, holding a six-pack of wine, lets himself in through the door that has been left ajar and following him are Greg and Anne. Anne must have met Greg at the pier. The three of them make their way up the stairs and stand in front of the painting. They stay spellbound before her masterpiece.

"Otto, is this gathering your doing?" She presses the old man's arm.

"Well, you're not the only mischief maker in this town, Miss Pia," he says. "You're going to be surprised by all the people who come through here tonight."

Soon Hernando Iglesio's there, carrying a tray of what looks like burritos wrapped in silvery paper. He sets them down on the food table next to the beer. Then comes Paul Wayne, bringing bottles of champagne and plastic cups, which he places on the table opposite the beer. He takes a plastic tablecloth with a red poinsettia design, paper plates and red and green napkins from a drawer in his bench and places them on his work table. Then he becomes interested in the work. He, too, gets lost in the painting, looking for himself.

The newly formed groups gather in front of the murals, gabbing in excitement with each other about the scenes, getting up close to them. Frances continues to sing her Christmas carols, amazed that the painting includes all who have come to see it. Even the mayor shows up with his kids Milla and Isabella. He tells Frances they want to thank the lady who painted the dolphins on the side of their house. At his prompting they begin to sing "Jingle Bells", then "Deck the Halls."

She imagines Nicola here with them. The crowd begins to sing with the children. In her mind's eye, Frances sees the birds fly and the banners of colors sway; she hears the seals bark a rhythmic beat, the whales whistle, the ravens crow, the cormorants swoop, the pigeons coo; the heron unwraps herself, and the land and the sea beam with aliveness on this winter night before Christmas.

Frances knows she's not alone in her song to the infant child. Thanks to Otto, her buddies have gathered in the studio. Wayne's singing and smiling. Sali and Bimi show up with two hundred samosas which they start to pass around. Frances dances with Russell. Umberto sets out his cream-filled *cornetti*, the ones she loves with patisserie cream. Pizzas arrive from the Café Trieste. More beer comes from Smitty's. Sausalito's handsome firemen strut in.

Chris and Yofe get everyone dancing. Peter is dancing with Valerie. Milla and Isabella do a *pas de deux*. Elisa plays the bongos. Valerie serves French hors d'oeuvres. The musicians from La Stella's, David and Stuart, move on into the studio playing bistro music all the way. Will from the photo shop shows up with his camera, taking pictures of the crowd and the mural. Paso Rio paints the scene. Rosalie blesses the mural and the day. Laurie gives grace to the event.

When Frances has drunk too much beer and fallen into Russell's loving arms, she sees Greg and Anne dancing. They are locked in an embrace, swaying to the music. Hernando is dancing with Officer Bentley. Otto's smiling, with joyful tears streaming down his old face. Tom and Millie open some Dom Pérignon. Peter and Barbara sway to the music. People dance into the night. For all she knows the old ones are here, too. She swears Papa Pia and Al Sterling are doing the mambo next to Anne and Greg.

Frances is dozing off with a big smile on her face as Anne

whispers goodnight and places a gentle kiss on her cheek. Frances reaches out for Anne's hand and places a kiss there.

"See you later Anne," she says, bringing her hand to her own lips to keep that Anne-feeling before she falls asleep.

•   •   •

When Frances wakes up, Russell's holding her face in his hands. Her eyes move toward his. His face glows warmly in the flickering light. It's silent in the two-story building, still dark. The rain has stopped. This must be the silence of eternity. The spotlights dim now. Candles flicker next to Styrofoam trays of Indian food. A bottle of red wine, half full, rests on the table. She adjusts herself to her surroundings, falling deeper into Russell's warm arms. The Queen chair where Anne sat earlier is empty. She continues her search for clues as to where she was, what has passed.

Confused, she stares at the murals for answers. They are luminous, buoyant with animals and children, parks and swings, and a pirate ship of fools. She looks at Russell, half-expecting he will break the silence. But instead he sits quietly, embracing her newness, her nakedness. He's looking at her as he might a beautiful child.

19

The Epiphany, January 6

Two weeks have passed since the Christmas Eve gathering in the studio, and now Frances is home on her boat, living again on the anchor with schools of fish circling beneath her vessel. The roll of gentle waves lulls her. She imagines spending this night sitting with a cup of hot tea in her hands, feeling at peace. Whenever has she allowed such a simple moment, she wonders. But soon the peaceful feeling evaporates with the steam of her imagined tea, as if the devil has something else in store. Frances stares at the thirty-foot mainsail rigging, imagining her boat at full sail with her at the helm. She can almost feel the wind on her face as the boat slices through the night.

Tonight at the Spinnaker Restaurant her work will be displayed officially, along with the unveiling of the new plans for a children's playground, and she has been invited as a guest of honor. She feels twitchy at the thought of being in the crowd, fearing that in the midst of the well-wishers she'll be suffocated.

Setting sail for a few hours, though risky in another way, seems safer. She can taste the salty wind on her lips.

From the deck of her boat she looks at her watch and then to the two boats nearest her anchor, Russell's on one side and Otto's on the other. The cabin lights mean they are still on board, tidying up before the evening festivities. She waits and counts her blessings, the gifts she's received. She does the *examen,* the prayerful review. She's grateful for the recovery of her old paintings that became a real art show, Anne's forgiveness, Otto's friendship, Russell's love, Paul's generosity, and the contentment in having completed these new works and in sharing them more publicly.

Awareness of this newly found space, however, makes her nervous, too. Frances looks at the main. She could hoist that sail singlehandedly but not now while Russell is still on his boat. She looks toward his anchorage and sees his shadow moving about. Not yet.

Yes, it's best to check the systems right here at anchor, and not when she's in the middle of the slot heading straight into the wind, she reminds herself.

I want to go alone and not invite Russell to go with me, she determines.

She wants this night to sail alone as some important ritual she can't yet name. Remembering the loving three-day tryst she had with him, she for a moment wonders if this cockamamie plan that she's formulating isn't self-sabotaging. She dismisses this.

She recites a checklist, the sailor's guide, as the litany to escape from this sudden doubt. *Hoist the sail to check the moving parts, put in a reef before leaving anchor. I must wait until they leave for the party.*

• • •

Frances goes below and sits on her berth, wraps her arms around her bosom, and waits, feeling the springy spongy bed of flowers beneath her feet. The sunflower eyes smile at her as she squishes her toes into them, the way Russell squished into her. Russell sent them by water taxi delivery to celebrate their lovemaking and their sail around the bay. The spongy garden carpet at her feet gives the boat an earthy smell. Her toes reach out of her sandals to grasp more of the petals, to hold onto him a bit longer. *Oh, so soft, like his feet.* A pang of grief slams into her when she thinks of leaving the touch of his soft feet, the elongated muscles in his neck, the way he cups her body, squishing into her, his affectionate pinches on her cheek. And what about the tango he does with his Franny? She realizes, *It's all too much. It's overwhelming.*

Then the memory of Nicola comes with the wind, bringing a pang of longing. She grips her sides, bending down, letting the blood rush toward her head and shake up those tired brain cells. Then she puts her fingers inside her blouse to squeeze his ashes. They said all loss is the same, but she doesn't buy that. This loss is inconsolable—a mother's loss that cracks her mind and heart like a lightning flash.

She bites down hard on her tongue to kick away the loss, the longing for the mutual love growing inside her. *I must set sail.*

Quietly, she slides back the hatch and climbs the companionway ladder to the upper deck, unclipping the snaps on the blue cover for the mainsail, folding it neatly below; then she checks the sheets are free of the boom. She won't take a chance on hoisting the sail to put in a reef while Russell and

Otto are still at anchorage—that will have to wait until she's out in the channel. More than likely that means she sails with a full sail. In other words she'll fly. *If need be, I'll take the main down completely and sail on the jib alone. I've done that bundles.*

Frances looks around as if she's a thief, sneaking away in the night. She looks at her watch; she looks at the tide tables, still a small window of time. The water is slack like a black stain this half hour before the tide changes. She imagines she's sailing on the ebb and out through the Golden Gate with the full moon guiding her path across the water. Frances becomes alert to Otto's moving shadow on his deck; he's preparing his skiff. She wakes up. Something is finally happening. His inflatable is closely held, taut to his ladder. Otto's bending now to get into his boat. She imagines she hears his joints creak as he bends and kneels to make the moves to get inside. She wants to avert her eyes to how old he has become, yet she wants to applaud the eighty-something-year-old's prowess. In the small boat he starts his engine, frees the line. He's heading toward her boat.

Her heart beats rapidly. She waits, slipping her hand through the opening in her blouse, clutching the blue satin pouch she keeps tucked into her bra, squeezing his ashes that attach to her heart of sorrow. Her fingers slip inside easily. She pinches the ashes, so soft and chalky between her rough fingers. Taking them to her nose she smells them and then places a dot on her forehead the way she always does on Ash Wednesday. She blows some ash into the cold night air. Then she squeezes the pouch shut when she hears the sound of an engine nearby. She jumps. Otto pulls up at her stern now.

"Otto, what's going on? You startled me," she says, shoving her hands in her pockets. In the night, his blue eyes are like the dark sunflower seeds.

"Frances, Frances," he says lovingly, his voice shaking away the weirdness in her. "The wine's waiting for us at the Spinnaker. Come with me." He gestures for her to hop in his boat.

"But I'm not ready," she says, "We will drink together later." She feels the bone dust still under her fingernails.

"*In vino veritas,*" he says. The truth is she wants him to go and she wants him to stay. She wants to tell him that she'll miss him, that she might never see him again if . . . if what? She wants to tell him that she loves their talks and the old-world knickers he wears and the smell of wool he carries in his gnarly body. A pang of sadness swells in her throat.

"What time is it? Is it almost time for the ebb?"

"In a half hour," he says. Then he turns toward the shore.

Only a half hour left and with so much to prepare she may not get out. She'll be trapped, confined. Even here! I may botch this.

"You look beautiful, Franny." Alarmed, she swivels around to see Russell at her stern. She hadn't even heard his engine. He had dipped his oars through the slack black water, rowing over to her boat.

One goes another comes, should she have been this lucky in another day? Maybe it's easier for relationships when we get old.

"A true bride," he says, reaching a hand toward hers.

"It still fits," she says girlishly. "I've saved it for this special occasion."

"Is that for me, Franny, for us tonight?" His face beams like a child. He moves forward, tying up his small boat to hers as if he's coming on board. She turns around, puts her hand up. She's conscious of standing there in her dress and veil, the one she wore when she took her final vows, the one she's saved and carried in the bottom of her valise all these years, the one in which she felt entirely whole as His bride.

She looks at Russell. She touches the front of the dress, But she has no memory of having put it on for the party or of having taken it out of the valise that she stores in the lazarette at the stern of her boat.

She wants him to come in to caress her, but she mustn't let him step inside. Not one inch closer. She feels heat rising from her low center up through her chest and neck onto her face. Her lips tremble. Now she wants him to come aboard and take her in his arms, to pull her body against his, to kiss her face with his soft petal lips, but she mustn't let him step on board.

"Come on-a my house, my house, I want to give you everything." Russell sings an old Rosemary Clooney song! She shifts her feet and dances in front of him with her arms rising, her hands twirling and her hips swaying. Her shoulders open and close, her lips moisten as she dances the seven veils.

"Heat and hotty totty too, my sweet spot, just for you," she sings aloud in response to him, swirling her wedding veil toward her lover as waves of fire rush through her center. *How is this coming down like this? He will hop aboard if I don't cast him off.* He's aroused too, she can tell, as he sways his thin waist and reaches out for her, beckoning her to jump into his boat with him.

She turns away, looking behind her where the main sail is sitting exposed.

"Just refolding the main after our sail around Angel Island and Tiburon," she says.

"Let's make love again right now, Franny. Here in the cockpit." He meets her eyes.

"Yes sir-ree," she manages. "But tonight, later, after the party when I'll dance the seven veils for you. Now get you off so a girl can dress up properly for the festivities."

"I like getting you off," he says.

"Get outa here," she laughs, freeing his line and tossing it to him.

"Are you blushing, Franny?"

She smoothes out her dress, running her hands over her breasts, down toward her waist and then over her pubis, her thighs and her butt, feeling the wetness between her legs. She throws a kiss toward her dear friend Russell, squinting again to see that he has moved beyond the marker, sufficiently away from her mooring. She can make out a shadow figure near the channel marker. It's too dark to see whether he has crossed over, but she must get going to make the ebb.

The silence is as black and reflective as the calm water under and around her boat. It reads like the end of a painting, the end of the novel of her life, filled with a space that invites her to sit in this simple white linen dress and drink her tea, holding the chalice of warm liquid, and receive this moment of life.

But she can't.

Checking the tide table against her watch, she makes the necessary adjustment for Richardson Bay. The turning is near. The slack is nearly over. The waters will soon aid her on out and under the Golden Gate. She secures her inflatable to the stern, places the rubber fenders in the lazarette, and pulls up the anchor before starting the engine. At first it sputters and chokes and then stalls out. *Damn!* She waits before she tries again, not wanting to flood the thing. She imagines a flooded engine. What then? The oars? No way.

Holding the tiller, she presses the flowers between her toes, remembering Russell saying, "Franny, you're blushing." Then Anne saying, "The Doms tend the dead." She relaxes and tries the throttle once more. It catches. Finally she's motoring out toward The Spinnaker Restaurant, feeling the mist on her cheeks. She hadn't expected fog on this cold January night, but she reminds herself that for her, fog has always been a gift from God.

She holds her breath, facing the fog-lit night, clutching the satin pouch which seems to whine to her when the sound of the first horn off the gate bellows a deep and haunting sound—*brooooooooooo droooooooooooooooooom*—to match her beating heart. She counts, *One, two,* then the great pause, ten seconds long. She waits to hear the second blast of a higher-pitched horn. Then another. A kind of symphony out on the bay with each horn speaking to the next, melting into the responding other. Their language soothes and scares her. Many a sailor's nightmare is to sail without visual clues from the sky and the land. She thinks of the opera, "The Flying Dutchman," where the sailor is cursed to roam the sea perpetually for seven years, only to be freed if a woman will love him truly and faithfully. *Oh dear, that's not me!* She shakes off the admonition and looks at the moon behind the fog, giving off its gauzy light like the tulle veil she wears on her head, knowing that the fog is her friend.

"You're not the winter moon I expected, with your icy glow laying down a silver path for me," she says to the moon, "but you're still giving light, though it's a softer light." Moistened by the fog, and in front of the now partially shadowed moon, a sliver of white light rests on her head. It's both a crescent and a shadow. Almost like an eclipse. *How odd this kind of fog is in the winter. Sailors beware!* The wind blows the great fog bank toward her. She ignores this warning, facing into the wind now, dousing the engine, jumping up onto the cabin house deck, and hoisting the main. Then she jumps down again to turn off the engine, hardly noticing the goose bumps rising on her bare arms. With the main sail up, she sails slowly through the channel past the Spinnaker Restaurant and the festivities. The town lies twinkling on her starboard side.

She's on course with the Golden Gate in sight. Finally it's safe to turn on her navigation lights, grateful for the quiet night in the channel. Not always so with cruisers or ferries and even ships heading out to sea from Oakland and Richmond. The wind, unrestricted by the hills, opens up her pores and enters her, seeming to cheer her on toward the black sea where she will fly.

She presses the bosom of the silky dress she wears, grateful for the warmth of the tweed skirt underneath. She puts her red coat around her shoulders as a cape. With one hand clutching the tiller and the other adjusting the white veil, she flies like a great winged bird. Gathering a bit more speed, she sails under the Gate, heading for the black patch of sea still visible in the distance.

The fog hasn't dampened her navigation, not yet. She will soon be able to see the lighthouse on her right at Point Bonita. She remembers today is the celebration of *Epiphania*, January 6, when the vision of God is revealed through the child. Is the aliveness she feels as the winged bride of the night a vision revealed? Or is it the other revelation: Russell loving her as she is? Or Anne loving her no matter what? She doesn't really know.

Sailing close-hauled on the wind, the mainsail is a perfect arc. The ebbing water pushes her out to sea, breathing in rolling crests beneath the hull. She touches her crown and veil, thinking she is truly thinly veiled, flowing between the magic of two worlds. Nothing is holding her back. The bride and her transfigured child of ashes are finally heading home together.

The boat is moving faster as she passes Point Bonita, where the fog becomes denser and low. She can barely make out the lights on the tower. The wind picks up and the swells toss her about. Straining at the tiller to maintain her course, she feels exhausted. She struggles with its weight and after an hour she tires. Her only choice is to heave to. She works fast to rig the boat so that the sail faces into the wind. Finally, when the boat has some stability against the wind and the swells, she rests on the floor of the cockpit with her coat as her blanket. With the boat wobbling back and forth like a giant cradle, her eyes flitter from side to side as her lids close. She nods off, dreaming she's dancing on the great sea of life. She sleeps as the boat keeps its spot on the open sea just beyond Point Bonita and the lighthouse.

Opening her eyes she finds herself on the cockpit floor with the soft feeling she has just been kissed on her cheek by Anne. But then she wonders if she's dead, and whether the boom hit her head and knocked her out. Is this heaven, where other souls like her spend glorious time dancing and stretching, waiting for God? All she knows is that she's lying in the center of a moonlit room which is her home. By volition or by grace, she has found the center of her being, no longer an outlier. She feels blessed here in this space in the middle of life, hanging out on the edges of the vast star-filled ceiling above her and the floating womb of the sea below. Life swims above and below her and she is at its center. It feels like eternity but by her watch and the rise of the moon from the horizon she's been out only an hour.

She rides with a rhythm inside her, kicking out her out-stretched limbs and rolling her shoulders to the beat of the drum while gentle riffs of water hit the sides of the boat. She rolls on her side with the steady joggle rocking back and forth.

Then she's drawn to a beam of light that flows in three strands from the full moon, now totally exposed. Three white beams of light make a direct line from the moon to her heart place. She opens and shuts her eyes in rapid succession. Still the lines of light are directed toward her heart where she places her hand, and then squints again at the bright moon held in its opaque sky like an infant glistening from its placenta.

"Am I nuts?" Frances asks the moon.

"Yes, go home, Frances." She hears this response clearly.

"Why did I think I had to leave my loved ones?"

"You don't."

A great feeling of relief fills her, brimming to fill her eyes with teardrops that glisten and fall onto her red coat reflecting in the moon. *I can live this life you've given me, dear Lord, and fully. I can sit in my cabin with a cup of hot tea in my hands and my loved ones nearby.* She reaches into her breast pouch and takes out the small bag, opens it, and kisses it. Then she releases the powdery ashes into the night. She watches as they fly in the gentle wind, now floating above her.

"Safe travels, Nic," she whispers. "You are free now."

She stands up and readies her sails and then jibes toward the Golden Gate, letting the winter hit her face.

She's heading back home.

Acknowledgments

I thank my teachers and coaches. First: Brooke Warner, my editor and publisher of *She Writes Press*. My creative writing instructors at SFSU: Nona Caspers, Maxine Chernoff, Camille Dungy, Junse Kim, and Dody Bellamy, who all read parts of *Anchor Out*.

And to my mentors in psychology: Jim Bugenthal and Jessica Broitman, who always had faith in me as a writer and psychotherapist.

I'm grateful for my first readers more than ten years ago: Kat Kroll, Ann Ludwig, and Susan Shaddick, who saw the beauty in my story and loved Frances, and who continue to support me.

I thank recent readers: Molly Giles, Brenda Gunn, Debra Turner and Leah De Nola. My Petaluma writer's group: Sue Salenger, Clarice Stasz, and Marsha Trent. And especially KathyAndrew, who has read all the iterations of this novel, including doing a final edit, as have Ann Ludwig and Susan Shaddick.

I thank Book Passages for its support and for introducing me to Molly Giles and Brooke Warner, the Mystery Writers Conference, and its first publishing seminar.

I thank Napa Valley Writers Conference 2008 and 2009, and Ehud Havazelet, who told me that even Mrs. Dalloway had a plan. That comment helped me to squeeze out just what Frances' intent was.

Gratitudes

Gratitude for Peter, my partner, who sustains me in sickness and in health. My son Peter and daughter-in-law Valerie, and my daughter Elisa. They not only guided me through my cancer but continue to support me in every way. The joy of Isabella and Milla, my granddaughters, during those first years of illness, taught me how to play again. Without their love and faith in me I would be lost, I'm sure. Thank you.

My sister, Cathy: I love you, and wonder at the way you had to be moved around by a big sister like me. I take glee in the many ways you have surpassed me.

My friends carry me through the days and nights of my life as we share this path. Kathy Andrew, Chris Durbin, Gay Galleher, Cheryl Krauter, Andrea Lichter, Ann Ludwig, Roberta Sapienza, Susan Shaddick, Sharmon Hilfinger, Joanne Vaccaro, Ingrid Volen, and so many others. I am so lucky.

I thank my floating consultants: Laurie Lynn Schubert, Guido, Henry, Kusuru and sailor Peter Sapienza. I bow to the small cafés in Sausalito: The Sartaj, Café di Vino, and The Taste of Rome who welcome their anchor out patrons who have taught me so much about living on the anchor. As I listen to their stories about the trials and tribulations of living anchor out, I know they are my teachers. They are awesome courageous people who are guided by the sea which can both hold them and toss them mercilessly. They are threatened by gale force winds, horrific swells, torrential rains, wild currents, anchors that pull out and send them adrift. They have learned both a willingness to surrender and to yield. And more.

I give gratitude to the Sausalito Parks and Rec for beautifying Sausalito and making the parks safe for children.

Remembrances

I'd like to acknowledge Chris Baty, the author of *No Plot? No Problem*. I met him at Book Passages one sunny day in 2004. Sitting outside, I was skimming the book he would soon present inside the bookstore. When he asked me if I liked it, he revealed his authorship. That summer I read the book with enthusiasm but it wasn't until October of the following year, after receiving a diagnosis of breast cancer, that I decided to write this novel.

On November 1, 2005, Frances emerged like Botticelli's Goddess. Venus on the half shell, emerging from the sea. She took me through the descent of her life, which paralleled my own current feelings of despair, having just received what I feared might be my own fall into death. She took me to the boat, living outside and waiting like the souls at the river Styx in *The Aenead*. From there I hung on for dear life, following her sins, and in the end when I finished on November 30, 2005, I had Frances setting sail through the Golden Gate, in a form of exhilarated suicide. An exulting and trembling ending!

That day, November 30, 2005, I put the pen down and nobly left the handwritten manuscript of fifty thousand words on my desk and drove with Peter, my husband, to Kaiser to undergo a surgery that would remove the cancer and tell me my fate, if that is even possible. I felt like a woman warrior without a shield—like Frances, who had accompanied me on this journey, as have other women with breast cancer.

From there I turned my attention to the spiritual realm to regain my faith, which I lost during this ordeal. This led me to Spirit Rock, a Buddhist Vipassana Center in Woodacre, California where I learned to meditate. But not only that, I learned to read the beautiful teachings of Buddhist teachers and to practice Loving Kindness, which have become part of my prayers. Then I met Mary Neill, a Dominican nun, who directs people like me. I became one of her people and once a month we meet to talk about what consoles me.

Our discussions not only have given me a return of my faith in the moment and in life, but also a way to examine within myself what it means to be human—some of which, Mary says, is being the patient donkey in Mary Oliver's poem, *The Poet Thinks About the Donkey,* who places one foot ahead of the other when he is not obediently waiting to be led.

Mary gives me the courage and the hope to be human, the courage to surrender to what is and to allow. I hope Frances' story portrays for you some of this struggle.

I'd like to mention my painting instructor, Fred Reichman, my first teacher, who brought me to Gottardo Piazonni, his first beloved teacher, a fine artist whose work still stuns me. I have used some historical facts about Piazzoni, whose paintings were moved from their first place, the old SF main library, to the de Young under much controversy. Fred was one who fought for them to stay at the old SF main library, which is now the beautiful Asian Art Museum of San Francisco.

And my grandfather, Nicola Della Piana, was not a painter but a handsome tailor from Italy, who worked at Jordan Marsh in Boston during World War II. He fathered me when I was an infant until my father returned home from the Philippines when I was two. Then Papa died. I've often regarded him as my first father.

Finally, I return to Cheryl Krauter, Nona Caspers, and Brooke Warner, whose attitudes encouraged me to publish. Each said in her own way that my original last chapter no longer worked, that Frances didn't have to die, but instead could go home to her beautiful life. For that I am relieved. Frances and I are both free to live.

About the Author

Barbara Sapienza is a retired clinical psychologist who practiced in San Francisco. At sixty-six she enrolled in the graduate program in Creative Writing at SFSU. She writes, paints, dances, practices taiji and meditation, and volunteers in a school program in Marin City. She lives in Sausalito with her husband and enjoys her granddaughters, Milla and Isa.

Author photo by Jay Daniel / Black Cat Studio

SELECTED TITLES FROM SHE WRITES PRESS

She Writes Press is an independent publishing company
founded to serve women writers everywhere.
Visit us at www.shewritespress.com.

A Drop In The Ocean: A Novel by Jenni Ogden. $16.95, 978-1-63152-026-6. When middle-aged Anna Fergusson's research lab is abruptly closed, she flees Boston to an island on Australia's Great Barrier Reef—where, amongst the seabirds, nesting turtles, and eccentric islanders, she finds a family and learns some bittersweet lessons about love.

A Cup of Redemption by Carole Bumpus. $16.95, 978-1-938314-90-2. Three women, each with their own secrets and shames, seek to make peace with their pasts and carve out new identities for themselves.

What is Found, What is Lost by Anne Leigh Parrish. $16.95, 978-1-938314-95-7. After her husband passes away, a series of family crises forces Freddie, a woman raised on religion, to confront long-held questions about her faith.

Fire & Water by Betsy Graziani Fasbinder. $16.95, 978-1-938314-14-8. Kate Murphy has always played by the rules—but when she meets charismatic artist Jake Bloom, she's forced to navigate the treacherous territory of passionate love, friendship, and family devotion.

The End of Miracles by Monica Starkman. $16.95, 978-1-63152-054-9. When a pregnancy following years of infertility ends in late miscarriage, Margo Kerber sinks into a depression—one that leads her, when she encounters a briefly unattended baby, to commit an unthinkable crime

Shelter Us by Laura Diamond. $16.95, 978-1-63152-970-2. Lawyer-turned-stay-at-home-mom Sarah Shaw is still struggling to find a steady happiness after the death of her infant daughter when she meets a young homeless mother and toddler she can't get out of her mind—and becomes determined to rescue them.